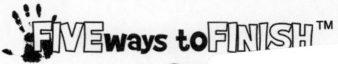

FIVE ways to FINISH™

MICK MORRIS Myth Solver

#5 Abominable Snowman... A Frozen Nightmare!

written by K.B. Brege
illustrated by D. Brege

ISBN 978-0-9774119-4-8

The trademark Five Ways to Finish® is registered in the U.S. Patent and Trademark Office.
Printed in the United States of America
First Printing Paperback edition – September 2009

Copyediting by Bethany Kalina, email: beschy@aol.com

Special acknowledgements to Mick, Katie, and Karl.

Printed by McNaughton & Gunn, Inc.
Saline, MI USA
August, 2009

This is dedicated to everyone who loves to laugh,
and you know who you are.

Table of Contents

#5 Abominable Snowman... A Frozen Nightmare!

Chapter One

"Okay, who left the backpack lying in the hall? Miiiicccck?" Mom yelled.

"It wasn't me, Mom…it was Harold. Hee, hee, hee," I laughed from upstairs.

"Oh, really? I didn't know the cat had a backpack." retorted Mom, "Pick it up, please."

I could hear her laughing under her breath, and that was my plan. If I could make my parents laugh when I did something wrong, then I knew I wouldn't get in as much trouble. But I still always wondered why mothers ask questions they already know the answers to. I slowly dragged myself back downstairs to pick it up, knowing if I didn't, she wouldn't be laughing anymore.

Once downstairs, I found Mom and Dad in the kitchen talking; they quickly looked up and stared at me.

"I came down to pick it up," I said as nice as I possibly could.

1

"It's not about the backpack," Dad smiled.

I couldn't believe what my dad began to tell me! We were going to Alaska! I began dancing around the kitchen; I was so excited.

Then I stopped dancing; I wondered-*why Alaska*? What myth could possibly be there? Then it hit me! The only myth that could possibly exist in that cold climate would be…

"NO!" I yelled aloud, not even realizing it while shaking my head.

Mom and Dad looked at me strangely and nodded, "yes."

"Really? The Abominable Snowman?" I asked.

It was true, over winter break we were going on a myth solving mission to a remote part of Alaska. The Uncover Station would film the cable show "Myth Solvers" and try to solve the myth of the Abominable Snowman, also known as the Yeti.

Even though it wasn't widespread knowledge that the Abominable Snowman had been seen in Alaska, there had been some recent reports in Skagway, Alaska, of people finding giant footprints in the snow. Animals were missing from farms, and trees were found pulled right out of the frozen ground by their roots. Some of the brush was found trampled, yet there was no explanation for any of it.

2

Worse than that, people would come back to their homes to find them ransacked and torn apart. Doors would be torn right off their hinges and every window shattered!

Police had been investigating, but there were never any clues, except for one – several long pieces of white fur left at the scene of the crime.

Rumors spread for years that the snow beast could've crossed over the ice bridge from Asia to Alaska. The exact same way humans moved to Alaska hundreds of years ago.

So what else could Myth Solvers do? It was our mission to solve one of the oldest and most mysterious myths of all time. What we didn't know was that it would be one of the biggest risk-taking missions we had ever been on.

Chapter Two

Screams pierced the night sky as a terrified woman ran into town! Her face was ghostly white with fear. She ran door to door, pounding her fists, while screaming "Abominable! Abominable! He here! We die! Save selves!!!" She would even yell things in her native language that nobody could understand.

Her long, black hair was snarled and tangled. Even though the temperature was a freezing five degrees, all she was wearing were her pajamas and no shoes! Besides her footprints in the snow, she left a small trail of blood.

Lights began to turn on in the tiny town of Skagway as her piercing screams began to wake everyone up!

"Abominable! Abominable! Death is coming!" she hollered as she ran hysterically toward the police headquarters!

Many of the townspeople shook their heads and turned their lights back out as they closed and locked their doors. This wasn't the first time this had happened.

When she arrived at the front of the Skagway Police Station, the woman frantically screamed something that could not be understood. An Officer came out and she collapsed into his arms.

"What is going on?" asked another Officer coming out to help.

"It's just Atka…guess we'll keep her again."

The police officers lifted the lifeless woman and carried her into the station. When they got her inside, they laid her down on a bench while one of the officers went to call the local doctor.

"Jeez, Bill, will you look at this?" asked an Officer.

"What, frostbite?" asked Bill.

"No, it's way worse than that…"

The Officer hung up the phone, and as he walked over to Atka he gasped at what he saw.

Chapter Three

When the plane took off I braced myself. I had a funny feeling in the pit of my stomach, and I was pretty sure that it wasn't from flying.

I knew this was just the beginning of our terrifying adventure. Plus, I had really gotten used to traveling in the Myth Mobile, the giant RV we took to our myth solving destinations. This time there was no choice.

I really don't mind flying. It is a fact that, to get to Alaska, you have to fly over active volcanoes. And when the plane comes in, even though the volcanoes are monitored by scientists, they could erupt at any second.

I had heard that, once before, a plane was flying over one of the active volcanoes, and the volcano suddenly erupted. It covered the plane in ash, and there was so much smoke engulfing the plane, the pilot couldn't see to safely land…so, well, you get the idea.

The thought sent shivers up and down my spine. It was one thing to chase myths, not knowing if they really exist, but volcanoes – we know they're real.

Especially since, last year, Mount Redoubt had erupted twice. It had sent a blast 65,000 feet straight up into the air. That's over 12 miles high! That part of Alaska had 'ash fall' of up to an eighth of an inch, and that's besides the sub-human cold temperatures, mounds of snow, wild animals, and icy glaciers!

The only reason I knew this was because we were studying volcanoes in science class. Then, of course, we had to make a model. I was never quite sure why teachers always wanted you to make models of things you just learned about. I guess they like them. Either that or they like their classrooms filled with stuff.

Chapter Four

I shook away my fears and began to think of the positives of Alaska, like the beauty and rugged wilderness. I was really lucky to be on this trip *and alive*, considering some of our close calls with myths in the past!

I decided to try to relax and continued reading my book about myths. It was my favorite book. I found it a long time ago, when my mom dragged my dad and I into an old antique store. It was at the bottom of a box filled with junk and covered with dust. It had a worn-out, brown leather cover, with an old button and a loop closure. There was no title on the front.

Inside, all it said was, "Cryptozoology." The book was filled with information on every myth that you had ever heard of, and then some.

As I began to turn the delicate, ancient, yellow pages, I came to Abominable. It said that the Abominable Snowman was originally discovered by scientists in the 1920's. It was believed to be an ape-like cryptid, originally sighted in the Himalayan mountain range by the Sherpas.

They were the people of that region. They called the beast "The Wild Man of the Snows." Many expeditions, dating as far back as the early 1800's, had tried to track it down, but with no luck.

Even a famous actor searched for the fearsome beast.

A rumor went around that the actor somehow smuggled a decaying hand, known as the "Pangboche Hand", back to the United States.

It was said to be a mummified hand of the Abominable Snowman, belonging to a monastery high in the mountains. When the hand was examined by scientists, they found that it was human-like – but not human! Then someone stole the bones, and it never turned up again.

"Human-like" made sense, since the beast was known to walk upright like a human. Throughout the years, many scientists have found unexplainable giant footprints and long, strange fur samples.

Abominable is said to be at least 15 feet tall, possibly weighing up to 2000 pounds. It is covered with thick fur and has ape-like arms, very similar to Bigfoot.

Some say it has white fur, and others say it's red. Somehow, the thought of this creature really frightened me.

Hours later we touched down safely in Juneau, Alaska. I breathed a huge sigh of relief and was happy to be on the ground.

I couldn't wait to see my best friend, Nathan. Nathan's dad, Miquel Juarez, was a Director for the Uncover Network and usually on the "Myth Solver Show." Since Nathan's parents were divorced, Nathan spent half his time with his dad.

I was also happy that my cousin Sissy wouldn't be along on this mission. I was tired of her acting so girly-girl and flirting with Nathan all the time. I knew that he liked her, too. It was something I should be happy about – my cousin and best friend liking each other, especially since Sissy had helped save the day on some of our past myth solving missions – but I just wasn't.

Nathan is my best friend, and she is my silly girl cousin, "Sissy the Serpent." Besides, pink isn't a color to be wearing while you are hunting down vicious myths!

Chapter Five

By the time we got checked into one of the hotels at the airport, it was really late at night. It didn't seem any different from any of the other airport hotels we had stayed in. The only thing I could tell about Alaska was that it was really, really cold.

When we got to our room, I found my way to the connecting room from my parents', threw on my pajamas, and plopped into bed. I was asleep in seconds.

It seemed like only minutes later when I was startled awake by a pounding on my parents' door. Scared, I jumped up and went into their room. My dad was already peering out the peephole asking who it was. That was one thing about my dad, he was super cautious when we traveled and he taught me to be as well.

I shuddered as I thought, *if he only new about some of our hair-raising close calls on past myth-solving missions*…like when Bigfoot exploded right before our very eyes, or Champ began climbing those rocks, coming after us, and even when we were chased through the museum by those horrible little gremlins! To think those gross little things could grow another body part in seconds!

"Well, hellooooo!" said my dad as he turned to look at me smiling, and slowly opened the door. "It's the abominable Nathan!"

There was my best friend Nathan, completely bundled up from head to toe in a giant parka, with fake fur framing his face and giant snow boots, holding a new snowboard.

We laughed so hard. Skinny Nathan looked like he was a giant marshmallow man!

"What? What? I plan on staying warm," he mumbled from his oversized coat.

"Yeah, Dude, warm is one thing…but that coat is enough to bake you!" I laughed. "Great to see you!"

We did our secret handshake with his giant glove on.

"Si," said a familiar voice from down the hallway. "I wondered how he could even walk in that coat!" The familiar Spanish voice was Nathan's dad.

We teased Nathan and all hugged. It was so great being together again. We talked about the craziness of being sent to Alaska and the possibility of an Abominable Snowman really existing.

Nathan showed us his new snowboard. It was totally cool and one of the hardest to find anywhere; it was from the famous ghost-hunting "Ghost Board Posse" team. It was even signed by them!

"It's for you, dude!" Nathan smiled.

"No way!" I shouted. "Are you kidding me? Thanks so much! How did you get this?"

"Uhhh…my dad has a few connections," said Nathan.

I thanked Mr. Juarez with a hug and high-fived Nathan.

It was by far the coolest snowboard I had ever seen. But, what I didn't know was that this snowboard would soon save my life.

14

Chapter Six

When they left the room, I quickly got ready, and we met the crew in the lobby. It was always like a homecoming seeing each other again.

Everybody was talking while we headed to the typical hotel dining room for breakfast. Once seated, we caught up on what we had been doing since the last time we were together in Dearborn, Michigan.

Dennis, being the expert that he was, began to tell us a totally frightening story about the Abominable Snowman...

By the time he was done with the story, we couldn't finish our breakfast. The story was awful! My stomach was turning; it began to make me wonder about Dennis. Had he been a Cryptozoologist before he became a Boom Operator?

I knew he had flown planes in the war, but was he once a cameraman on the story he had just told us about? Why did he know so much about all of these myths? What made a man that was so big and so strong so afraid of these mythical beasts, yet so knowledgeable about them? All I knew was that I was going to have to post his scary story on the Mick Morris website when I got home.

"So, Mick, like when do you think your cousin will be here?" asked Nathan.

I almost choked on my waffle!

"Uhh...," I said while clearing my throat. "You mean Sissy?" Of course, I knew that he meant Sissy.

There was no other cousin on our myth solving missions. I wondered for a moment why my cousin Aidan, who was totally cool, couldn't be on these missions.

Yeah, I thought to myself, *why couldn't that side of the family be into myth solving?* I would have to think about asking my mom if Aidan could come along next time.

"I don't think she's coming this time," I said, trying to contain my excitement.

"Oh," Nathan replied, clearly unhappy.

I felt bad about that, but I cheered him up by secretly discussing our plans for finding the Abominable Snowman.

After breakfast we checked out of our hotel. We were heading to the town where the filming would actually take place.

Once outside, I was thrilled to see a giant rented RV. It wasn't the Myth Mobile, but it would do. The crew had an RV, too, and another rented truck filled with gear.

It was a long and bumpy ride through the rugged Alaskan terrain. As beautiful as it was, there was an eerie feel to it, knowing there could possibly be a terrifying, man-eating beast out there.

The sky was a bright blue, and there were thick towering pine trees lining the two lanes of the twisting, curving road. We were amazed by all the animals you could see from the road; everything from deer, moose, elk, skunks, and porcupine, to bears. Yeah, I said bears. We could see them; big ones, too.

It made me kind of wonder, as big as the bears were, could they be what people had seen and mistaken for Abominable?

When the temporary Myth Mobile would pass a clearing, we could see solid white, icy mountains of snow that seemed to go on forever. The mountains and shimmering glaciers were beautiful. This was the true wilderness.

I knew that, on this mission, we couldn't wander far, or we would freeze to death in this remote, cold place. The occasional howling of a wolf was kind of freaky and made me think about being safe out there.

When we finally got to our destination, Skagway, it looked like a sight out of a movie. It was a small, old mining

17

town. It had old wood buildings lining both sides of the street that divided the town.

Back in 1897, there was a gold mining boom, and in just a few months, the town went from one cabin to a population of 20 thousand people! It had been filled with outlaws and criminals, who had come looking for gold.

One really bad guy, known as Soapy Smith, ran the town and robbed everyone. But a man named Frank Reid shot and killed Soapy, and he became the town hero.

The Yukon Gold Rush ended a few years after that, and those that remained kept the town going. Now, it wasn't hard to miss the hotel, because it had a giant sign on it that just said, "Hotel."

As we began to unload our luggage, we were startled when a screaming woman came running down the street toward us!

Chapter Seven

We dropped our bags and ran over to the crew. The woman was now pulling on one of the crew member's jackets while screaming, "Help me! Help me! Abominable! Snow beast! Myth Solvers help! Get snow beast!"

"Where? Where is a snow beast?" asked my Dad, trying to calm the hysterical woman down.

"I show, I show!" She said, shaking and crying.

Seconds later, the police arrived. Dad chatted with them, while Mom tried to talk to the woman. The crew knew something was going on, and they instantly began readying their gear.

"Could it have been a bear?" I asked. "They seem to be pretty big and white out here."

The woman instantly came over to me and got right in front of my face. She had a bizarre way about her. Her long black hair was a mess, and her wrinkled clothes looked sort of like gypsy-fashion.

She glared at me. I felt like I couldn't move. I could only look at her straight in the eye. She lifted a finger and shook it back and forth. I followed it with my eyes.

"Noooo beeeearrrr. Noooo beeeearrrr! Hoooge foot prieeennt! Hoooge foot prieeennt! ABOMINABLE!!!!" she yelled.

"Atka, that's enough!" insisted one of the police officers.

Dad finished quietly chatting with the police, and then told my mom they were going to take a helicopter to see if they could find anything.

"...It will give me a good idea as to where we can start filming, too," continued Dad.

"No electric bird! No electric bird!" The woman screamed at the top of her lungs. Then she took off running toward the end of the town.

"What? What just happened with that Eskimo woman? Did we do something?" Dennis asked the police.

"Gotta warn you, Sir, folks in these parts don't like the term Eskimo; it's pretty much frowned upon. The preferred term is Inuit," said the Police Officer quietly to our group.

"Oh, sorry about that," Dennis apologized.

"No problem. And about Atka, it's nothing new. We're not so sure about her. She moved here about a year ago from her native village, I guess. It seems to happen on almost a daily basis lately."

They continued to explain that the mysterious woman would not ride in anything that flew; no planes or helicopters. Her name, Atka, meant "one lives and knows things," or some people say, it means "guardian spirit."

He went on to say that she had claimed, for the last few months, to see Abominable. She told them that the beast was after her for something from a past life. They had been trying to run a background check on her, but couldn't come up with anything.

"Just be careful. There might be something to all of this," Mom said warily as Dad left for the helicopter station with the police.

Chapter Eight

Nathan and I were helping unload the luggage, when Nathan leaned over to me and said quietly in a funny, scary sounding voice, "Hoooge foot prieeennt! Hoooge foot prieeennt!"

We couldn't help but crack up. I was laughing so hard, I had to stop to wipe the tears away. As I glanced down the street, I could see the woman! She was near a tree, just staring at us! I nudged Nathan and pointed, but by then she had quickly disappeared.

"What?" Nathan asked.

"Ahhh…nothing, maybe just a glare from the sun bouncing off the ice," I said.

As we trudged up the hotel steps, the owner greeted us. He was a very thin man in black jeans and an old plaid sports jacket. He had thinning gray hair and wore a name tag that said, 'I'm the owner. Call me Sam'. We entered the old white hotel. It had a big round dome sitting at the top of it that looked like something from Russia.

Once inside, I instantly got the chills. Lining the lobby walls were animal skins and stuffed, dead animals! It was like an instant flashback of our horrifying adventure in Port Henry, New York.

Nathan and I looked around as he said, "Are you thinking what I'm thinking?"

"Champ," I agreed while nodding.

Nathan had the same freaked out look on his face as we remembered the terrifying 'Shapeshifter' that chased us back to Port Henry, where we had barely made it out alive!

"I gather you boys don't like dead animals much?" wheezed the voice of the owner.

We both shook our heads, "no."

"I don't think that they are used to seeing so many dead ones in one place!" joked Mom.

"I understand. It's kind of my hobby," said Sam. "Alaska is known for its hunting and fishing."

Mom nodded and gave her fake smile that I know so well. She finished checking everyone in while we helped the crew bring in the luggage.

The creepiness had already started. That eerie feeling you get when you know something is going to happen... It was the same creepy feeling I always get before a terrifying myth solving mission.

Chapter Nine

Nathan and I got to share a room again. It was a strange old room, decorated with antique furniture. There were two brass twin beds, an old wooden dresser, a small roll-top desk and a couple of chairs, and flowery wallpaper.

The bathrooms were down the hall, outside of the room, which was odd. I guess that's how things were in the olden days. At least we got to share a room; it made our Myth Solving a lot easier, and it was a lot more fun.

"Wow! I'm bursting at the seams! Can you believe it, Mick?!" asked Nathan in a loud whisper.

"What? The gross dead animals again?" I asked, as I began to unpack.

"No…although that's really creepy, too…But there's just NO WAY that woman could've been faking it! Un-be-lievable! There has to be an Abominable Snowman!" said Nathan, as he quickly went through his suitcase.

"I don't know. I believed in the other myths, but I'm not too sure about this one. That woman seemed a little bit too wiggy for me," I stated.

"Maybe, I don't know…it sure seemed like she was totally terrified to me!" replied Nathan. "Hey, I hope you like your snowboard. It's for your birthday – wish I could've been at your party…but, you know, living in Los Angeles and all…"

"Are you kidding? I love it! Yeah, must be rough living in the land of movies and stars" I joked.

"Hey, it's not all that cool out there. Kinda plastic, if you know what I mean," joked Nathan, as he did a ridiculous pose while pulling the sides of his face back.

"Oh yeah, I know!" I said, as I posed back.

We both fell on the floor, cracking up.

"This board is totally cool! How did you get it, anyway?"

"The Ghost Board Posse had to meet in LA before their international tour started. So, my dad had some of his peeps get them for us. He has a couple connections, you know?" smiled Nathan.

"Thanks so much, man!" I said.

"C'mon, whadda ya say we head out and try to find her and maybe put our boards to a little use?"

"Find who?" I asked, as I admired my new board.

"The crazy lady," said Nathan, as he pointed his fingers at his ears and made the crazy sign while crossing his eyes. It was all I could do not to fall off the bed laughing again.

"Okay, yeah, let's see if we can get her to talk to us."

We quickly packed our backpacks with charged walkie-talkies, compasses, and all the supplies we thought we would need. Little did I know there were no supplies that could help us on the most dangerous mission – ever!

Chapter Ten

We headed down the creaky hotel stairs. The place was old, I mean really old. When we headed into the lobby, it was easy to imagine the mining boomtown days in the past, with crowds coming and going in the hotel lobby.

You could almost hear the piano player pounding out some honky-tonk music on the worn-out ivory keys. The place must've been filled with people in Victorian clothes and miners coming in, happily shouting that they had struck it rich with gold from the Yukon.

We turned down the narrow hallway and found our way to the tiny conference room. Mom and the crew were already going over plans for filming.

"Is it okay if Nathan and I check out the little town for awhile?" I asked Mom.

"Okay, just don't wander far, and bundle up. Don't be gone long. I have a surprise coming for you!"

"A surprise? Wonder what it is, but that's awesome!" I said to Nathan as we left the hotel.

The minute we walked outside, a rush of freezing cold air hit us in the face. Skagway was known for its winds, and this was a big one.

The place was breathtaking. Huge snow-capped mountains surrounded the small old city. It looked like a picture from a painting.

We quickly put on our gloves and headed toward the spot where the screaming woman had been. There was a little general store nearby, so we figured that would be the best place to find out where she lived. We couldn't have been more wrong.

The place was filled with everything from Alaskan souvenirs to fishing poles and mining picks, from groceries to shoes and batteries. You name it, they had it.

"Help you boys?" asked an elderly woman's voice from behind us.

"Oh, hello," I said, startled. "We were wondering if you might know where the gypsy, I mean Indian, woman that was so upset from earlier today, lives."

"You think you fancy TV people can come up here to our peaceful town and get everyone riled up about some fake Abominable Snowman – DON'T YOU?!" She yelled. "Well let me tell you something, you little…."

"Henrietta!" a man's voice snapped.

Nathan and I spun around to see a burly man, completely bundled up and covered in snow, holding a spear with a bloody fish on the end and walking our way.

"We don't know no woman like that…now go on – git, unless you plan to spend your money here!" he said.

"Uh…uh, we were just leaving!" said Nathan, as we backed out of the store while the couple walked toward us.

Bam! Once outside, we both tumbled backward over a snowbank! The door of the old store slammed shut.

'Ha, ha, haaahhhh!' came from behind us.

Oh, no! That laugh! There could only be one like it on the entire planet, I thought to myself! *But nooooo! This couldn't be happening…not again!*

Chapter Eleven

Nathan jumped up as fast as he could while dusting himself off.

There it was, standing there in full-blown pink winter gear from head-to-toe!

"Sissy! Uh...hi!" said Nathan happily.

"Hi! Who is that?" asked Sissy

We turned to see the old woman's face move away from the window, while her hand turned the "Open" sign to "Closed."

"Okay, that was random," I stated.

"No kidding! Oh, well, anyway... Surprise!" she said as she jumped back and threw her arms out to the side.

"Surprise what?" I asked.

"Surprise me! That's what!" she squealed with delight. "I told your mom not to tell you guys that I was coming so it would be a big surprise!"

"You're the surprise?" I asked, scrunching my face.

"Yep! My dad and I just got here."

"Lame," I said under my breath.

"What?" asked Sissy.

"Great, yeah, like great!" I replied. I knew I had to act happy the minute I saw Nathan beaming like a lovesick puppy dog. I couldn't understand what he liked about my cousin, who now looked like Ms. Disgusting in pukey pink.

"Yeah, really cool that you're here!" said Nathan.

"Yeah, cool, but we've gotta check this out before it's time to head back. So…like, see ya later, Sissy," I said as I began to move toward the other stores.

"Uh-uh-uh, did you forget about the aliens, Bigfoot, Champ, Gremlins, and how about…?" she continued.

"Okay, I get it. C'mon then!"

Sissy was smart. She knew she was part of our myth solving team, no matter how I felt about it. She also knew that when people act the way the people in the store did – trying to get rid of us – then they're hiding something, and she wasn't about to miss it.

Nathan filled Sissy in on what had happened, as we headed down the street toward another souvenir store.

This time it was run by Inuit, so we hoped they would know something about the woman named Atka.

When we asked about her, we got the same rude reply and were almost thrown out of another store! Only this time, the owners had fear on their faces…a fear that we would soon encounter!

Chapter Twelve

We knew there was only one thing to do; we had to find the strange woman's house on our own. We started to head to the end of the town where the woman had come running from. As we trudged through the snow, we were startled by honking behind us.

It was the crew!

"Where might you three be heading?" asked Dennis.

"We were…uh…we were…uh…souvenir shopping…," I stuttered.

"Yeah, I need to find some boots in pink. So I'm dragging these guys with me," smiled Sissy, as she practically knocked me out of the way to get to Dennis.

"I see," replied Dennis. "You know your Dad is back from the search, and we're heading to interview Atka.

It was all I could do to keep from acting too excited, even though we wanted to get to her first. At least we could see what she had to say.

"Want to come along?"

"Yeah!" we shouted in unison. As they opened the back door, we jumped in.

"Hinkleson to base," Dennis said in the walkie-talkie. "We got 'em."

"Oh, good. We'll meet you there," said Mom.

I quickly unzipped my backpack and realized I had forgotten to turn on my walkie-talkie...I knew I was in trouble now. I quickly flipped the switch...but it was too late. My mom was going to be mad.

Not only did I make her worry about where we were in this strange little town, but I could've messed up their whole filming schedule. When they're on location, it means they have to stick to a schedule, and things have to get done quickly.

As the truck turned down a small, tree lined, curvy road...the feeling in the pit of my stomach went away. I knew I would no longer be in trouble, when my parents saw what was ahead.

Chapter Thirteen

It was Atka's house, and what a sight the place was. It was a small, old-fashioned, white house in really bad condition. Shutters were half hanging off, and junk was everywhere!

Even creepier, the entire place had strange drawings and symbols painted in dark red on it. Sketchy images, of what looked like versions of an Abominable Snowman, covered the house.

There were animal skulls and weird charm things hanging on the porch, and an old beat up couch. In the corner of the porch, was a big drum; everywhere you looked was an odd mess!

But the weirdest was right in the middle of the front yard. There was a huge sign that read, "Atka's voice speaks the truth. He is here. Save yourself – he is here!"

"Do you think she's okay?" asked Sissy.

"Depends on what you call okay," I replied.

"Based on the looks of her house – I would say no," added Nathan.

We exited the truck, quietly and carefully following Dennis, Brett, and James as we made our way toward the creepy front porch. The place had an eerie, deserted feel to it, but there were fresh footprints in the snow.

"Anybody home?" yelled Dennis. There was no answer. Just total silence in the cold outdoors, except for the eerie breeze wafting through the enormous pine trees, and the crunching of the snow under our feet.

"Well, only one thing to do…," stated Dennis, as he stopped walking and turned to look at us.

"What's that?" I asked, shivering.

"Knock on the door," smirked Dennis.

Brett and James laughed as Sissy, Nathan, and I tried to join in on Dennis' odd sense of humor. But I could tell by the looks on their faces that they knew something was not quite right.

It was almost like we could feel something bizarre and frightening was about to happen. Maybe because we had been on so many myth solving missions together…

Discovering the existence of those wild myths, and barely making it out alive, or maybe it was because we had never ventured into such a cold, remote area as this before. Either way, this house was so disturbing, it gave me the chills. And this was only the beginning…

Chapter Fourteen

The loud sound of engines startled us! We turned to see the rented myth mobiles pulling into the narrow driveway.

We walked over to them to greet our parents.

"Okay, this would be an interesting place to start filming, since we didn't see anything from the helicopter," said Dad climbing out of the RV.

I went around to the other side to take what I had coming to me…

"Hi Mom." I said sheepishly.

"Don't 'Hi, Mom,' me, Mister! You broke our biggest rule! You know you can't wander the streets of strange cities without your walkie-talkies on!" scolded Mom.

"But we were just in front of the hotel…"

"No excuses, Mick! And would you look at this place?" She said, forgetting about our conversation as she stared in awe.

Whew! I thought to myself, *thanks to the bizarre house, I was in the clear*.

"We were just about to get permission to interview her," said James.

Mom and Dad joined James as they walked up onto the old, white front porch and gently knocked.

The front door slowly creaked open, but no one was there.

"Helllooooo…," said Mom softly.

Suddenly, a screaming woman wearing a white fur polar bear rug came running from the back of the house with a giant metal wrench in her hand!

When she realized who we were, she dropped the wrench and fell to her knees, pounding her fists into the snow and muttering something in a different language.

Shocked, we stood there for a moment. Before we could move, she stood up and began to point up to the sky while yelling.

It wasn't clear what she was saying, but then she stopped, and she began to yell in English…

"He come for me. You must go. You leave now."

My parents and the crew quickly surrounded her, calming her down and talking to her about Abominable. They explained that they wanted to film her story.

By the time they were finished, my mother had gotten a thermos out of the RV, had a cup of hot cocoa in her hands, and had convinced her to let them film her.

That was it. Set-up for filming began in her odd house, which was just as weird inside as outside.

She had quite a few pictures of Abominable from books and seemed to be interested in audio engineering books as well. When I asked her about her interests, she walked right up to me and gazed into my eyes.

It really startled me. She was right in my face! Then she practically read my mind as she said, "You no go look for Abominable! YOU NO GO!!!" She screamed, and everybody froze.

Chapter Fifteen

All I could manage to do was to shake my head "no." It was like I was in some kind of trance for a second.

Luckily, the crew finished setting up, and Mom came to put her on the set. Little by little they began to interview her about her Abominable encounters.

"She really creeps me out," whispered Sissy.

"You think?" I asked.

"Yeah, but now's our chance to investigate a little," said Nathan.

We began to move toward the front door, I could feel Atka still staring at me.

"We're just going to check things out," I said casually.

"NOOOOOO!!!" Atka screamed at the top of her lungs. She came running over to me, grabbed my hand, and kneeled down as she began chanting.

My parents swiftly pulled her away, telling her everything was fine, and that we would be right outside.

"Wow! That was weird! Kind of over the top – don't
cha think?" said Sissy.

"Sissy!" snapped Uncle Hayden, at her
outspokenness.

I couldn't help but snicker at Sissy getting in trouble.

"You do have those walkie-talkies, don't you,
Mick?" asked Mom, a bit concerned.

"Uh, yeah, all set, Mom," I said as Sissy, Nathan,
and I went outside as fast as we could.

Once outside, I showed Sissy and Nathan what Atka
had shoved into my hand when she was kneeling and
chanting.

It was some kind of ancient amulet, carved out of
green stone, on a worn brown leather cord. On it there was a
carving of strange circular designs, with markings around it.

"Well," I said, as I put the strange necklace on,
"hopefully this will bring us good luck in finding out if this
Abominable myth is real or not," not knowing just how
much luck we were going to need!

Now it's your turn! You get to decide which ending of the book you would like to read. There are *'Five Ways to Finish™'* this book; just pick the ending and turn to that page. Then, when you're finished with that ending, come back to read the other endings!

1) For a normal ending, go to page………….....43

2) For a very scary ending, go to page……….....90

3) For a sizeable shrunken ending, go to page....117

4) For a rearranged reverse ending, go to page…143

5) For a tell-tale tabloid ending, go to page…….153

Chapter One - Normal

Nathan had the idea that we should go around to the back of the house. We put on our warm gloves and crept around the back. I couldn't tell if it was the cold winter air that was giving me the chills, or if it was the thought of what we would do if we really did encounter this beast.

We stayed close together, and before long, I had forgotten about being afraid while we enjoyed the wild landscape of Alaska.

Atka's backyard was long and rolling with a frozen creek running through it. As we wandered into the dense forest, we did a quick walkie-talkie check. Apparently, everything was going well with the filming. Atka was busy telling her wild stories about Abominable coming after her.

Sissy was ahead of us, when she suddenly stopped and waved us over.

"What's this?" she whispered.

There was a clump of matted, white fur hanging on one of the branches.

"Could be from a white wolf," exclaimed Nathan.

"A wolf?!" panicked Sissy.

"Too high of a branch," I said.

"A polar bear?" questioned Nathan.

"Polar bears?! Here? So close?" shrieked Sissy.

"There's no water here. They like water," I answered.

"How about just a big rabbit?" asked Sissy.

We looked at her, not sure if she was joking or not. That was kinda what bugged me about her; sometimes she seemed smart, other times she was ridiculous.

We examined the fur. It was unlike anything we had ever seen! It was thick and matted, almost crunchy. But even scarier was, when we looked down at the ground, we discovered a gigantic footprint!

Sissy gasped! Nathan and I shook our heads in amazement while we kneeled down to check it out.

"Maybe Atka isn't lying after all," said Sissy.

The footprint had to be at least 2 feet long – IT WAS ENORMOUS. I fumbled in my backpack for my camera, while Nathan looked for his measuring tape. We couldn't believe the size of it!

We were excited to get back and tell everyone what we had found. It was really true! There was some kind of massive beast roaming Alaska…and now we had proof!

As we stood up, eager to head back to the house, a low sounding growl filled the air. It seemed like the trees above us were beginning to shake!

"Oh no, what was that?" asked Sissy.

I didn't know, I could only guess...I thought, *we could make a mad dash back to the house*, but when I turned to look back, I saw we had wandered farther than I realized! We were now out in the Alaskan wilderness...and some growling beast was just a few feet away!

Chapter Two - Normal

"Oh, no! Now what?" cried Sissy.

"Not sure, but we can't stay here. There's something coming, and I don't think it's a rabbit!" I said.

We began to run in the opposite direction of the sound. We were darting through a thick forest of huge trees. Sissy began to run ahead of us.

"Sissy, we have to stay together!" I yelled. I thought about using the walkie-talkie, but there was no time. The terrifying growl was getting louder and louder. We were trying to stay together.

We could hear the faint sound of tree limbs cracking and brush breaking behind us!

I wanted to look back to see what it was, but we had to keep moving, and now the snow was getting deeper, making it really hard to keep running.

After a while, we came to a clearing. We bent over, breathing heavily, trying to catch our breath.

Nathan and I knew what we had to do. I quickly unhooked my walkie-talkie from my belt, while Nathan dug in his backpack for a compass, because now we were lost.

"Mick to Mom, Mic…," I stopped.

"Mick, what was that?" asked Sissy, shaking. I didn't know if she was shivering from cold or from fear, or from both.

"I don't know, maybe a polar bear." I said, while Nathan and I tried to figure out which direction we had come from.

"I don't think that was a polar bear," said Nathan.

I gave him a look, and he knew what I meant. I was only saying "polar bear" because I didn't want Sissy to be anymore frightened…than she already was.

"Ok…k…kay, I see that look Mick! Don't try to pr…pr…protect me! In case you forgot, I was on all those other mi…mi…missions with you," she stuttered, her teeth chattering.

"Yeah, I know, but something tells me this mission is going to be a little bit worse," I said, watching as Nathan held up the compass.

"Wh…wh…what do you mean?"

There was no more time to talk! The horrifying sounds began again, and the loudest, most ghastly roar that we had ever heard seemed to be coming our way!

Chapter Three - Normal

We hadn't gotten an answer on the walkie-talkie, and we began to run again. It seemed like we were either running through thick masses of trees or slipping across ice ponds.

"Look! Over there!" shouted Nathan.

Far away in the distance, we could see a small wooden building sitting on the side of a ravine. I stopped for a second, pulling my binoculars out of my backpack. Sure enough, it was a small cabin!

"It's our only hope!" I yelled.

But, when I looked at the ground, I realized that we were making it super easy for whatever gruesome beast this was to follow us. We were leaving our footprints in the snow!

"It's been following our tracks!"

Seconds later, there was another ferocious growl, but oddly enough, it seemed further back.

"Wait, look!" said Nathan, "A frozen creek!"

I had no idea how he could tell that, but he was right. About 10 feet away from us was a frozen, winding creek. It looked like it led right in the direction of the cabin.

We decided that, in order to throw the beast off of our trail, we were a going to have to trick him. We quickly split up, running in different directions and in circles, and then following our tracks back to confuse him. We made sure that we didn't wander too far away from each other.

Then we carefully tested the creek making extra sure it was frozen. We cautiously stayed by the sides as we slowly skated toward the cabin. Even though our strides left brushes in the light snow, it was hard to tell they were footprints.

We had gone quite a distance and hadn't heard any howling. We stopped for a second to check out where the cabin was, only to realize that things had now only gotten worse…way worse!

Chapter Four - Normal

The small winding creek was coming to an end...only to lead into a giant bay. The cabin was across the bay, sitting on the side of a hill. In order to get to the cabin, we would have to cross the frozen bay!

"I'm tired and freezing!" whined Sissy. "This is horrible, and I want to go back!"

"I know, so do I, but I'm afraid those sounds might be the Abominable Snowman," I said, while trying the walkie-talkie again. "Mick to Mom, Mick to Mom, Mick to Dad, Mick to Myth Solver Show...Mick to anybody...pleaasssseee!"

"I've got an idea!" said Nathan, as he pulled his snowboard off his back. "What if we use our boards and push ourselves across the ice? Sissy can ride with me on mine. They will totally glide on the ice!"

It was a fantastic idea, and, in this situation, I wasn't even going to think about Sissy and Nathan and whether they liked each other or not.

I pulled my board off my back. We hopped on them, sticking close together while helping Sissy balance. We began to glide across the frozen water!

The closer we got to the cabin; we began to realize that, what had looked like blue ice was really blue water! And even worse than that was the fact that we could hear the howling sounds again in the distance!

Chapter Five - Normal

It was a huge bay of freezing blue water that led out to the ocean!

We didn't know what to do! We knew we couldn't stop and stand on the ice! Especially with water ahead, we didn't know how thick or thin it was! We slowed down and looked around. We couldn't go back the way we came, and we couldn't go forward either!

"Wait! What's that?" yelled Nathan, as he slowed down a bit to grab my binoculars.

"Look! Look! It looks like a person – just below the cabin, on the side of the hill! And it looks like he is getting into a boat!"

"Over here! Over here!" Sissy began screaming at the top of her lungs.

"Shhhhh! Are you crazy???" Do you want that horrible beast that's chasing us to get here first?" I snapped.

"Well, how in the world do you think that guy will see us from way over here? Huh?" insisted Sissy.

"Will you two stop it? This is no time to fight…hold on, hold on…look at this," said Nathan, handing me the binoculars.

"He's coming our way!" I said, as I began to wave frantically.

"Yeah, but, come to think of it, he could be some kind of crazy person living way out here. I forgot that I am not supposed to talk to strangers!" whined Sissy.

"It's either that, or you can have a chat with the Abominable…who doesn't sound like he's too far away, either," I replied, trying to keep my cool. My patience with Sissy was running out.

"Okay, Mr. Smarty Pants…but there is just one problem," Sissy replied.

"What's that?"

"How is this man going to get his boat to us? We can't walk on thin ice, and we can't swim out to him either – WE'LL FREEZE TO DEATH!"

"She's right," said Nathan.

I looked through the binoculars at the man, who was now headed toward us.

"I don't think we're going to have to worry about it," I said excitedly, as I handed the binoculars back to Nathan.

Chapter Six - Normal

"What now?! Did the Abominable get him? Tell me what's happening!" cried Sissy, scrunching her eyes shut and almost tumbling off the board.

"Pay attention, and no!" I said, as I pointed to the man in the boat, "He's in an amphibious boat, one that can ride on all types of terrain – water, land, EVEN ICE!"

He was nearing the edge of the ice, which was about 70 feet from us. It was the coolest vehicle I had ever seen.

Suddenly, the frightening howls began again. This time, it seemed like they weren't behind us. Instead, the sounds seemed to be coming from in front of us!

"That's weird!" said Nathan. "It's almost like Abominable is circling around us!"

All we could hope for was that this horrible creature was far enough away, and that this man could save us! I was scared out of my mind! On all of the other Myth Solving Missions, I somehow knew we would be safe…but this time I wasn't so sure.

As the amphibious boat neared, we continued moving together, watching and shivering.

The boat was only about 30 feet away on the ice. We didn't know how thin or thick the ice was, we only knew, if it broke through the ice, we would, too! We slowly began to inch our way toward the man and the boat.

"Get back!" He hollered angrily. "I'll come there. Don't come any further out!" Seconds later, he pulled the boat right up next to us, as he made a slow turn.

"Hurry up! Jump in!" he instructed.

We quickly jumped in! I fell face first into the boat, while the man was focused on turning it and heading back to land.

"What in the world are you kids doing out here?" he asked as he gunned the engine.

I managed to sit up to see that he was a tall, thin man with a rough face. He was clearly the rugged type, dressed from head to toe in outdoor gear. He didn't look like the kind of mountain man you would expect find in Alaska.

"We, uh, wandered off and kind of got lost," I answered.

I wasn't sure if I should share our horrifying myth experience with him, but before I could finish...

"You three are really lucky! Abominable is close! Hold on tight!"

And at that instant, the boat began moving so fast it was almost airborne. It felt like we were flying! We held on for our lives!

Chapter Seven - Normal

Seconds later, the boat pulled into a small dock. We quickly followed him up the snowy hill to the cabin.

"Mick, we don't know this guy…do you think…?" asked Sissy quietly.

"It's this or Abominable, and, somehow, I feel safer with him."

"Well, I don't feel safe either way," Sissy stated, sharply glaring at me.

We walked into the man's cabin, and I was happy to see that it appeared to be pretty normal. It had the total rustic look, with dark wood throughout the small cabin. There was even a crackling fire in the fireplace. It felt cozy, and, to my relief, there were no signs of animal heads anywhere…which seemed kind of strange, considering every other place in Alaska seemed to have them.

In fact, it didn't look like he lived here very long. There was a small kitchen area, and a room that looked like a big office, with lots of equipment, like some kind of storage room. He quickly walked to that door, shut and locked it. I couldn't wait to find out what this man was doing way out here by himself.

"Hi, I'm Mick Morris," I said, as I extended my hand to shake his. "We are with the Myth Solver Show that's filming in town."

"I'm Nathan, Nathan Juarez."

"Cecilia…and you are not some insane mountain axe murderer or anything like that, are you?" interrupted Sissy.

Nathan and I groaned and rolled our eyes.

"Well, you never know!" snapped Sissy.

"Not today. I'm John Gooding."

I was relieved that he wasn't angry, considering Sissy's blunt rudeness.

"I'm actually…a…a…a hunter – yep, a hunter…tracking probably the same thing that you're looking for," He replied as he walked into the kitchen, filled a teapot, and put it on the stove.

"Abominable?!" Nathan and I yelled in unison, so excited, we could hardly contain ourselves.

"You got it. Been here a few years, looking for that beast. Word came down that he crossed the ice bridge, and I headed here; now you know, and I know, he's right out there! I've been…"

But there was no more time for talking. The ominous howls began again – this time they were louder than ever! In fact, it sounded like they were right outside the cabin!

Chapter Eight - Normal

Our eyes grew huge, and we didn't move. The man put his finger up to his mouth, telling us to be quiet, as he quickly went to turn off the lights and close the curtains. He directed us to get down on the floor behind the couch.

"It's nearby. This is the closest it has ever been to the cabin. I'm going to go out and have a look. You three stay here, in case I need help. And don't touch anything!" he said.

We nodded and crouched down behind the couch, silently. We were terrified as the howls grew louder and louder.

The man grabbed what looked like some type of tranquilizer gun from the corner, zipped his jacket back up, then slowly and carefully opened the door and slipped outside.

"Now what are we going to do?" asked Sissy.

"We have to get a handle on our fear!" I said. "This is a beast. We've had encounters like this before. We can take this thing!" I snapped. "Besides, we haven't even seen it yet! It might not be so huge."

"Mick's right," agreed Nathan.

"Are you kidding me? The size of those footprints and the loudness of those growls…THEY DON'T CALL IT ABOMINABLE BECAUSE IT'S THE SIZE OF A KITTY!" insisted Sissy.

"Shhhhhh, I agree. Somehow we have to get back to town! This time I think we need to tell our parents. Come to think of it, they are probably super worried about us by now!"

I reached for my walkie-talkie and clicked it on, I kept my fingers crossed – it worked!

"Mick to mom, Mick to mom…," I whispered.

"Heeeelllloooo, Sweet Pea," said an odd sounding voice from the walkie-talkie."

I knew it wasn't my mother's voice, besides my mother has never, ever, ever, called me Sweet Pea!

"Who is this?" I asked.

"Ha, ha, ha, ha, ha, ha!" Laughter boomed through the walkie-talkie, and instantly I knew that it was Dennis.

"Dennis, it's Mick!"

"I know it's you. What's up?" he asked.

In a way, I was glad that it was Dennis, but then I thought that he might be madder at us than my mom.

"You kids need something at the hotel? Put it on room service," he chuckled.

"We're not at the hotel," I whispered. It seemed like the groans outside had stopped, and all was silent – which was even more frightening.

"Your mother thinks you're at the hotel. Where are you? Oh, don't tell me that you're out…"

But it was too late; something started to pound violently on the back of the cabin! Now I knew – we were doomed!

Chapter Nine - Normal

Dennis was in a panic on the set. He knew we were in trouble and realized he couldn't alert our parents. He also knew that somehow, he was going to have to save us.

He quickly moved to another area of the house and tried to walkie-talkie us again, but this time, there was no answer.

His only hope was to figure out where we were. He flipped another one of the walkie-talkie switches and, sure enough, it glowed.

He quickly went to his cell phone. Luckily, he could connect to the GPS system in the walkie-talkie. Dennis was somewhat relieved, but knew he would have to work fast. This was one time that the Abominable Snowman wasn't going to hurt anyone!

He walked back to the set, finding that the break was ending. The crew was getting ready to film more of Atka. They had already had quite a time getting anything that made any sense out of her.

Atka would ramble on in her strange accent about the snow beast eating her home and silly things, like how she knew it wanted to marry her.

Many of the crew thought that she was just crazy, and her stories were so bizarre, that she had to be making them up.

Dennis quickly pulled James to the side, letting him know what was going on. James Brunk was totally cool, and you could count on him for anything. He was a laid back jazz musician. He would play clubs, when he wasn't on a filming job. Dennis and James had been friends since High School.

Next, Dennis approached my mom and dad. "I hate to break this to you, but we are having a bit of sound trouble. I believe we are going to need a piece of equipment for my boom microphone to wrap up this last segment."

"Oh, I wondered about that," said Mom quietly, as she moved away from Atka to talk to Dennis. "She either whispers her stories, or yells them, doesn't she?"

My dad joined them in the conversation and decided it would be a good time to call lunch. Mom picked up the walkie-talkie, and, just as she was about to use it, Dennis bumped into her and knocked it to the floor.

"Oh darn! So sorry, guess I will need to get another one of those in town, too," he stated.

"Can you call Mick when you do?" Mom asked Dennis.

"I...er...I just talked to them. I'll check in on them at the hotel," Dennis replied.

"Great," said Mom.

Dennis rushed out to the truck and headed to town. He drove straight to the helicopter rental. He was going to try to follow the GPS signal; hoping that it wouldn't be too late.

Chapter Ten - Normal

Thuds filled the air! They seemed to be moving toward the front door!

"Oh, no!" cried Sissy.

"Grab a harpoon off the wall!" I instructed.

Immediately, each one of us grabbed a giant whale harpoon. We didn't care what John Gooding said, we had to protect ourselves!

The gruesome howling started again! We crouched back down behind the sofa. I was hoping that I would be able to shoot the harpoon, and when I looked at it, I noticed it still had a price tag hanging on it.

Seconds later, the sound of breaking glass filled the air! Abominable had broken one of the windows! I had to look to see what was going on!

Sure enough, a giant, white, furry arm was flailing about! It had to be the size of a Sumo wrestler's leg! It was enormous! I shuddered looking at it! From what I could tell, it had long, curved claws at the end of each of its gigantic hands; the kind of claws that could tear you apart in an instant! It was groping around, almost like it was trying to figure out how to reach the door handle!

"Nathan, we have to try to stab its arm or something!" I whispered loudly.

Nathan carefully looked up as the growling continued, while the beast's arm smashed the rest of the glass out of the window.

"Are you crazy?" he asked, crouching back down.

"Well, we can't just sit here, let him break in and offer him some hot cocoa!" I snapped back, out of fear.

It felt like the entire cabin was shaking! The beast moved away from the window and to the front door; and it was pounding on it with all of his might!

"C'mon, we can sneak out the back!" said Nathan.

"No way, we're safer here," I argued.

"How do you figure?" he snapped.

Just then, a shrill whistle filled the house! It made us all jump! It seemed like it was as loud as a train; it was ear piercing!

It was the tea pot on the stove. It had begun boiling. It was the loudest teapot that I had ever heard!

But surprisingly the beast instantly stopped howling. The sound of shattering glass stopped, and there was silence – except for the shrill whistle of the teapot.

We sat huddled together for a moment completely freaked out.

Then, the worst that could happen did. The door knob slowly turned, and the door creaked open!

Chapter Eleven - Normal

Just as Sissy was about to scream, Nathan and I quickly covered her mouth. If this beast was getting into the house, we were going to put up the fight of our lives.

We trembled with fear, knowing what we had to do. We carefully lifted our harpoons getting ready to spring from the couch and take aim at the ferocious beast until…

"BAMMMM!!!!" There was a loud thud! The Abominable must've broken down the door!

We stared at each other for a second, then I slowly peeked my head around…

"It's John!" I screamed, while jumping up and running to the door.

Sissy and Nathan quickly followed, we pulled John Gooding in and quickly closed and bolted the door.

His clothes were all torn and shredded. We tried to wake him, but he was unconscious….slowly, he began to wake up.

Sissy ran and turned off the loud, shrill whistle of the tea pot and brought him a glass of cold water. Nathan and I tried to move him over to the couch.

"Wha? Wha? Where am I?" he mumbled. Then he screamed as he jumped up and knocked us to the floor.

"Ohhhhh…," he moaned when he realized where he was, while looking around. "I'm home, and I'm safe." He took a few sips of water and sat back down on the couch as he slowly began to explain what had happened.

"I almost caught Abominable, but then something went wrong with my tranquilizer gun…it got caught in my net. When I started to run from the beast, it followed me back to the cabin!" He stopped for a moment to catch his breath.

"But…but…the beast was just at the cabin door," said Sissy confused.

"I mean, oh…oh, I feel sick, I'm confused," said John, as he held his hand to his head and fell back on the couch.

"That's okay, take it easy," I said.

Nathan and I moved away, quietly chatting about how we thought John was delirious, and that the beast was probably lurking outside the cabin. We couldn't sit around any longer – we had to get help.

When we suggested to John that we call for help, he completely disagreed. He seemed to instantly feel better, in fact, he started to get angry as he insisted we needed to capture Abominable without any other help…but it was too late – the whir of a helicopter was now above the cabin.

When I told John that I had used our walkie-talkies to call for help, his face turned bright red, and he became furious!

"He's my beast, and I'll discover him! Not your stinking "Myth Solver Show!" he screamed.

John Gooding looked like he was ready to hurt someone!

Chapter Twelve - Normal

Nathan and I tried to reason with him; this beast was too big and dangerous, and we couldn't capture him on our own, without help.

But he wouldn't speak to us. He was so upset, he unlocked the mysterious secret room, went in, and slammed the door behind him.

Moments later, the helicopter landed in a clearing right outside the cabin. We looked out the window to see Dennis running up to the door. We rushed out to meet him, and were shocked to see massive Abominable footprints surrounding the house!

"You kids should not be out here alone!" Dennis yelled.

"Shhhhh…Abominable will hear you!" whispered Sissy.

"Abominable?" questioned Dennis.

"Yeah, look at the footprints!" Nathan said.

"Does my mom know we're here?" I asked.

"No, I didn't tell her – but we've got to get back, and now!" said Dennis, as he bent over to take a closer look at the footprints. "We're on a two hour break. James will keep everyone cool. I told them we needed a part for the microphone."

"That's great," I said, a bit relieved.

This wasn't the first time Dennis Hinkelson had helped us out of tight spot and James Brunk, too.

We insisted Dennis take a quick second to meet John Gooding, as we quickly led him into the cabin.

Dennis was surprised that there was such a beautiful cabin out in the middle of nowhere. We knocked on the door to the mysterious room, but there was no answer.

We pleaded with John to come with us.

"It's way too dangerous to stay here alone," I said, talking into the door.

"Go away! I need to rest!" was the angry reply from the other side of the door.

We begged Dennis to stay, explaining how this man had saved our lives.

"Sorry kids, we have to get that chopper back and now," insisted Dennis.

We left the cabin, making sure we locked the door as we followed Dennis to the helicopter. He had flown them in the war and was a master at it.

"How'd you know how to find us?" I asked as we buckled up.

"Your GPS on your walkie-talkie," Dennis replied.

Dennis was quiet, it was clear that something was bothering him, but he wouldn't say what it was.

"I hope that Mr. Gooding will be okay," said Sissy worriedly, "and this is the first time our myth solving mission has ended so badly."

I quickly shot her a look – before we'd have to explain all the other missions to Dennis.

The helicopter took off swiftly. As we lifted into the freezing cold blue sky I wondered why the huge Abominable prints in the snow seemed to come to an abrupt ending around the cabin.

Could there be some kind of Abominable Snowman lair near John Gooding's cabin? Was there more than one Abominable? Would they get him now that they found his cabin?

The helicopter moved fast, jarring us back and forth. It was a wild ride over the frozen terrain.

Seconds later we touched down…that's when it occurred to me, we had only wandered about a half hour away…Which made sense, because that meant the Abominable was really close to town…and even closer to Atka's house!

Chapter Thirteen - Normal

Once back on the set, Mom and Dad were happy to see us and said we looked tired, cold and hungry. Mom wondered why we didn't have lunch at the hotel; she assumed that we had been out snowboarding.

We didn't say yes or no, either way, it was always so much easier when parents assumed things. She was right about one thing – we were starving. We quickly chowed on the huge table of delicious catered food.

One thing about being on location, the craft services, as they called them, always had tons of delicious food. We couldn't eat fast enough, and for a moment, forgot all about our terrifying experience.

When everyone was finished eating, the crew began to get ready to film again. Nathan, Sissy and I moved to another room and began to relax as we chatted about how we were going to help solve the Abominable myth, now that we knew he existed.

A little later a police officer arrived on the set. He introduced himself as Sergeant Cooper. He held up a backpack clip and asked if it belonged to any of us.

It looked familiar. I quickly ran over to my backpack and checked the side of it. My backpack clip was gone!

"Yes Sir, that's mine," I stated timidly, as I began to reach for it.

The Sergeant quickly pulled it toward him and asked, "Have you children been together all day?"

"Yes," we said, nodding our heads.

"Then you three children are wanted for breaking and entering," he said, as he pulled out a warrant for our arrest.

"What?!" shouted my Mom, as horror filled our parents' faces. They immediately began to ask what was going on, while at the same time defending us.

"This is ridiculous!" said Nathan's dad.

Then Dennis pushed his way forward through the crowd, "I just picked these kids up out there, and they did not break into that man's house!"

"You were with them?" asked the Sergeant.

Mom and Dad immediately glared at Dennis.

"It's not what you think!" Dennis stated, trying to defend himself.

"What man's house?!" Mom hollered. She was really furious now, and everyone was completely confused.

"Then you, Sir, will need to come to the station with us as well," said the Sergeant.

76

People started shuffling everywhere. Dennis moved over to James Brunk and said something to him secretly. The crew was told to quickly pack up the set by the second Police Officer.

They instructed the crew that there would be no filming, and we were not allowed on the premises until this issue was resolved.

It was total chaos as the crew packed up the equipment as fast as they could.

Nathan, Sissy, Dennis, and I were now being escorted to a police car, while our parents got into the RV to follow us to the station. It was the worst thing that could happen! We were under arrest for something we didn't do!

Chapter Fourteen - Normal

The minute the police car pulled out of Atka's driveway and headed down the road, James Brunk quietly explained what was going on to the crew. They nodded while continuing to pack up, as James and Brett jumped into the truck and took off down the road.

"Where go camera men? No more picture Atka?" asked Atka suspiciously, as she watched James and Brett drive away.

The crew told her they were going to the Police Station, knowing not to tell anyone where they were really heading.

James and Brett turned down a side road so that they wouldn't be seen, but by the time they got to the helicopter rental, it was closed.

James knocked on the door, and when the owner answered, he pleaded with him to take them up.

"Can't it's dusk, gonna be dark soon – no way, can't do it," the man said.

"Just a 10 minute trip – I promise," begged James.

The pilot said "no." Until, Brett pulled out a 100 dollar bill and waved it in the man's face.

Within seconds they were lifting into the sky headed toward the cabin. James was now following the map on his phone to the GPS Dennis had hidden inside John Gooding's cabin.

Once they landed, James told the pilot to keep it running. They would be back in two minutes.

Luckily, James could reach inside the cabin to unlock the door through the broken window, but trying to get into the secret room was another story.

"Not a bad crib," said James.

"No kidding, for being out in the middle of nowhere. Kind of makes you wonder, huh?" said Brett, as he tried the door to the mysterious room, but it was locked. They decided they would have to break it down. They knew they could go to jail for breaking and entering. According to Dennis, it was the only way they could help prove everyone's innocence.

They picked up a heavy wooden table that was made out of a tree stump and rammed it into the door.

The door flew open! Sure enough, sitting right inside the room was a gigantic fake Abominable arm!

Chapter Fifteen - Normal

"RRRiinnngg, RRRiinngg, RRRiinngg…"

"Hello?" Atka answered her phone in a hushed voice.

"I told you never to call here!" she continued harshly, without any accent at all. "Yeah, the police got 'em and are taking them to the station now…you better have this one sealed up. These people aren't dummies…especially those nosey kids!"

"Are you ready?" barked John Gooding, on the other end of the phone.

"As ready as I'll ever be, you just better make this work!" snapped Atka as she slammed down the phone. She walked into the bathroom and began to rat her hair and tear her clothes.

This was going to be their only chance. Atka knew they needed to get the "Myth Solver Show" out of town. She knew they would never leave without first investigating the myth of the Abominable Snowman.

So, she and her partner in crime, John Gooding, had to create an evil plan – to make them believe that there was an actual Abominable Snowman.

She grinned as she thought about how well it had all worked; how they had lured Mick, Nathan, and Sissy to John Gooding's house with their fake sound effects through hidden speakers…a perfect trap to get those sneaky kids arrested!

Next in the plan, while the parents were busy getting their kids out of jail, was to act like Abominable was still terrorizing the town! This would give them just enough time to rob some homes!

What could be a better cover up than a fake myth? She laughed to herself, *Destroying everything in its path, while stealing jewelry and valuables! Boom! Just that easy!*

Then, once the "Myth Solver Show" was getting kicked out of Skagway, they would sneak out at the same time! With no tracks…except fake Abominable Snowman tracks; she couldn't have been prouder of herself and her wicked plan!

She was just about to apply fake blood to her face and arms, when she thought she heard something at her back door…then there was silence…but seconds later, it sounded like her door was getting kicked in! Then she heard a loud, scary animal growl!

Chapter Sixteen - Normal

"John! I just talked to you!" she hollered while walking into the kitchen. "What are you doing here? I told you…Oh, and you're in costume too. Isn't that nice? But you are supposed to be at the police station pressing charges on those kids, so those idiots will get out of here, and we can finish robbing this town, you fool! We can't do it right now!"

The towering beast was silent for a moment as Atka walked toward him.

She pulled over a kitchen chair, stood on it and grabbed the giant white head while pulling on the fur.

"Yeah, okay, great costume. Now take this silly mask off and get over to the police station and press charges!" She screamed into its face.

"RRRRGGGHHHHHH!" The hideous beast screamed right back at her!

"AAAGGGHHHHH!" Atka screamed in the beast's face!

It was the real Abominable! In one swift move the Abominable swatted her and sent her flying across the kitchen. She hit the wall and fell to the floor. Atka lay still in the corner of the room, not moving.

Immediately, Abominable went to the table of food and began shoving it into his mouth. While the beast was busy eating, Atka slowly and quietly managed to crawl to the other room.

Within seconds, she was out the front door and heading toward the police station. This time, she wasn't screaming, she was running so fast she could hardly breathe, and this time the blood on her arm was real!

Chapter Seventeen - Normal

Once we arrived at the police station, we were escorted in and shocked that we were going to be finger printed. I felt like a criminal – but I would never commit any kind of crime!

John Gooding was sitting in one of the chairs!

"These kids?" asked an Officer.

John Gooding nodded.

"Wait a minute! Mr. Gooding what are you trying to do here? You saved us from Abominable!" I yelled.

"Yeah, you, you…wait a minute," agreed Sissy.

"Abominable? How ridiculous! There's no such thing!" snickered John Gooding.

"How stupid!" I yelled.

"Mick!" snapped Mom.

"Sissy, Nathan, remember when he stuttered and said that Abominable followed him back to the cabin?" I asked.

"Yeah, I remember! That's when you said you suddenly felt sick!" Sissy yelled, while pointing at John Gooding.

"Because...yeah, now everything makes sense! You knew we were almost on to you, and it would have been impossible for the beast to get to the cabin before you!" insisted Nathan.

"Wait, wait just a minute here!" said Dad.

Then Mom and Dad, Uncle Hayden, and Mr. Juarez went from arguing with the police, to asking us and John Gooding questions. It was total confusion, until finally Mr. Juarez unclipped his bull horn – that he used on the set – and yelled, "QUIET!!!"

Everyone was silent while he instructed us to talk, one at a time.

"First of all, Mick Morris, what on earth were you doing in this man's home?" asked Mom.

But before long, everyone was shouting again...until the Police Station door flew open. Wind and snow came gusting into the police station.

Then, unexpectedly Atka collapsed through the doorway onto the floor!

"Not this scene again!" exclaimed one of the Officers, "Atka? Are you alright?"

But Atka lay still, not moving!

"She's bleeding!" yelled Mom.

The Police Officers ran over to her, to see if she was alright and helped her up...Atka slowly looked at John

Gooding and said, "The joke's on us…The Abominable Snowman is real!" and passed out.

Chapter Eighteen - Normal

Suddenly, Dad's cell phone began ringing.

"Hello...Yes, you're kidding me! No way! Okay, uh-huh...You got it? Great – will do!" said Dad, as he clicked off his phone, winked at me, and then pulled the Chief of Police into another office to talk.

When they came back out of the office, the Chief of Police said, "Book him."

"Whaaaat?" cried Mom. "What did you say to him?" she asked my Dad.

"Not him!" said the Chief of Police, as an Officer began to walk toward me. "Him!" he said, as he pointed to John Gooding.

"What? Are you insane? These little monsters broke into my home claiming there was an Abominable Snowman chasing them...what in the world is wrong with you?" hollered John Gooding, while standing up and backing toward the door.

Atka woke up again and began yelling that there was a real Abominable...

"Uhhh…May I ask what happened to your accent?" questioned one of the officers.

And just as she began to get up to escape, the door flew open again – but this time a giant Abominable Snowman arm reached in!

"Arrest me! I am guilty…it was all a scheme! John Gooding and I were robbing people, pretending that there was a real Abominable!!! And there is!!! Look! Aggggghhhh!!! Help me!!!" she wailed, as she ran into the arms of a Police Officer.

At that exact moment, Brett and James walked in laughing and holding the fake Abominable arm!

They also had some giant speakers and a huge fake Abominable foot on a stick for making footprints!

Immediately, Atka and John Gooding tried to escape from the Police, but they grabbed them, put their hands behind their backs and cuffed them!

Atka kept screaming that there was a real Abominable and someone had to believe her, but by now, everyone just laughed.

We told our story to the police and were free to go.

It turned out that Atka – whose real name was Anna Louter, along with and her husband Brody, aka 'John Gooding,' were wanted throughout the state of Alaska for robbery. They even stole the amphibious boat!

We were escorted back to the hotel. Nathan, Sissy, and I couldn't believe what a wild time it had been and how freaky the two criminals were. We chatted about how we could've been in more danger with them than with a real Abominable. We also laughed about how the Louters should've been actors instead of thieves!

We were really disappointed, too, that we hadn't solved the myth.

In the middle of the night, I woke up to what sounded like some strange growling...I got up and looked out the hotel window. For a brief moment, I could've sworn that I had seen a giant furry white beast wandering through the woods...but I realized I was probably just dreaming and went back to sleep.

The End

Chapter One - Scary

We wandered around to the back of Atka's house, only to find a lot of snow-covered junk in her back yard.

"Look at this old dogsled," said Nathan, knocking a pile of snow off of it.

"Pretty cool, but old," I replied.

"Yeah, like Atka. Besides, what good is a dogsled if you don't have any dogs?" questioned Sissy sarcastically.

She had a point. Yet, it was one of those moments when she was being a bit mean.

Nathan quickly asked if she liked dogs.

"I love dogs!" said Sissy, as she batted her eyes at Nathan.

"That's a lie!" I said calling her out, while jumping in on their flirty conversation.

Instantly, I realized I shouldn't have, when they both glared at me.

"Oh, well, okay...maybe now you do, like dogs – whatever. Either way, let's get myth solving," I said, as I began to walk down a long skinny path. It was in-between huge pine trees leading away from Atka's backyard.

I walked ahead, as the two of them lagged behind me, talking and laughing...*that's just great!* I thought to myself... until I looked down and saw gigantic huge footprints leading away from the path!

Chapter Two - Scary

"Look at this!" I yelled.

"You gotta be kidding me!" stated Nathan, as he ran up to see. "And I thought Atka was just a crazy lady!"

"Okay, those are enormous, maybe we should head back to the house," said Sissy nervously.

"You can if you want to. If it's cool with you, Nathan and I will keep going," I said, secretly hoping Nathan would agree and Sissy would head back.

"C'mon Nathan, let's see where they go!" I said, as I started to follow the massive footprints.

"Maybe we should make sure that Sissy gets back to the house safely," Nathan replied.

I knew he was right, and I had no other choice.

"Forget it! I'm a Myth Solver, too! I'm coming along!" snapped Sissy with her hands on her hips.

Although, I would've enjoyed just being with my best friend, I guess it was good to have another person along, and Sissy was always a major help.

We moved into the icy brush, sticking close together as we followed the winding path of footprints, while at the same time, looking for clues.

They were pretty easy to follow. Whatever made them, appeared to be so huge, it had carved out a path by crushing everything in its way.

We had been walking for quite awhile, and we began to wonder if we had gone too far into this mysterious, unknown wilderness.

Then the worst that could happen – did. I wasn't watching where I was going, and there was a thin layer of ice covering a giant hole. The next thing I knew, I slipped and fell into it!

I couldn't stop! I was falling out of control! It was a long tunnel…and I was sliding further and further down! It felt like a tube slide at a water park – but this one was no fun, it was cold, dark, icy, and scary!

The next thing I knew, I heard Nathan screaming! He had been walking closely behind me. He must've fallen in, too!

We were both rapidly sliding though the narrow tunnel! It twisted and turned, there was no stopping! The longer it got, the faster we went – I had never been so frightened in my entire life!

Chapter Three - Scary

"Oh, noooooo!!!" Sissy screamed, as she just barely stopped herself from slipping into the deep hole!

"Mick! Nathan!" she bent over and yelled down into it, but she knew we couldn't hear her, even though she could hear our frightened screams going down deeper and deeper!

Sissy didn't know what to do…she wondered if she should run back to the house to get help. But we had walked a long way on the trampled path looking for the Abominable Snowman…what if she ran into him – alone?! She paced for a few moments, not knowing what to do.

Suddenly, we stopped screaming. She slowly kneeled down next to the opening and yelled at the top of her lungs into the hole, "Mick!!! Nathan!!!"

For a moment, there was silence. Her heart raced, she thought this time we had really done it! Sissy realized that we had wandered too far, and now we were…

"Sissy! Can you hear me?"

She thought she was hearing things…it sounded like my voice yelling into a cardboard tube. She shook her head.

"Siiiisssssssyyyyy!" I hollered.

"Mick, Nathan! I can hear you! Are you okay?" she shouted back excitedly.

"Yeah, we're okay...you aren't going to believe this!" Nathan yelled.

Not being one to be kept wondering, she slowly dangled her legs over the edge of the hole, took a deep breath, scooted closer, and pushed herself into the icy slide!

As she flew down the twisting icy tunnel, she screamed with terror, realizing it wasn't any fun at all!

When she got to the end, she flew out onto the hard ice floor, bumping into us...immediately, she wished that she would have stayed at the top.

Chapter Four - Scary

"Oh, my gosh! That was awful!" she said, trying to sit up and catch her breath.

"Why did you come down here?" I asked angrily.

"I'm a Myth Solver, too, ya know!" Sissy said, half-heartedly straightening her jacket.

"You should've gone for help!" I exclaimed.

Sissy couldn't argue, all she could do was look around the cave in disgust!

The frozen ice cave was light enough to see because of the reflecting ice. To our astonishment, it was filled with some of the most ghastly sights!

Everywhere we looked there were animals in giant ice blocks! It was a hideous site. Some of them looked like they had been frozen in action, either yelling or fighting for their lives!

It was totally gross! There were stacks of bones piled high, and animal scraps and fur everywhere! The smell of rotting things was almost making us sick to our stomachs.

"We need to get out of here, now!" insisted Nathan.

There were three different paths in the frozen cave. We didn't know which way to go. Nathan quickly unzipped his backpack. He found his special device that could tell us which way air could be coming into the cave. It might give us a better chance of escaping from this horrible trap we had fallen into.

"C'mon, looks like we should go this way!" he said.

"I think I'm gonna throw up!" said Sissy.

"Take a breath and stick close to us! Don't look anywhere but straight ahead," I said.

We got on either side of Sissy, staying close together, as we carefully began to find our way out of the horrible cave.

Once we got far enough past the horrible site, we could see where some light was coming in. We made our way past enormous ice formations, and began to walk faster, being extremely careful not to slip on the ice.

Luckily, the ice we were walking on was scratched up enough to give us some traction.

Finally, we could see the entrance to the tunnel! We moved to the sides of the icy cave, just in case some horrible beast decided to come home!

We slowly inched our way forward, moving very cautiously. "We're almost out of here!" I whispered, trying to hide how scared I was.

As soon as we got closer to the front, a terrifying grunting and snorting immediately filled the air!

"Get back!" I said

We quickly threw ourselves against the cave wall and waited for a few seconds for the terrifying noise to stop.

"What is that?" asked Sissy breathlessly.

"Something big, that's all I know…maybe an animal? I said.

"Maybe…Abominable?" suggested Nathan quietly.

We looked at each other, our eyes wide open and our faces pale white with fear.

"Maybe," I said quietly.

When the frightening sound stopped, we began to move forward.

But when we got to the opening of the cave, we shuddered with fear! It the most frightening site we had ever, ever seen!

Chapter Five - Scary

Just 15 feet, directly in front of us was the largest, most hideous creature you could imagine! It made Champ in Lake Champlain seem like a bath toy, and Gremlins at the museum seem like stuffed animals, compared to the size and ferociousness of this beast!

It stood almost 20 feet tall and had to weigh at least 2000 pounds! It had ugly, matted, dirty-white fur that stood on end, covering its enormous body!

Its head was huge, with evil glowing red eyes and a massive mouth and huge sharp teeth…almost like the teeth you see on TV during Shark Week! Even more frightening were its mammoth hands, with big ugly, bluish-black leathery fingers and long dirty, yellowish, cracked claws that came to a razor sharp point!

"Abom…Abom…inable," I gasped.

But worse than its hideous looks, was what it was doing! It was holding onto some kind of dead furry thing and dipping it into the freezing water…like it was making a popsicle!

We stood staring in shock and disbelief!

It was like we were spellbound, watching this dreadful site!

Now we knew how all the animals ended up in frozen ice blocks! This brutal creature would catch his prey and then dip them to death!

I didn't even want to think about what he did later, but by the looks of his cave, it wasn't pretty! I snapped myself out of it and began to look for a way out of his terrifying lair…but now, it was too late!

Chapter Six - Scary

Abominable saw us! He immediately stopped what he was doing, dropped the frozen block and threw his hands angrily up in the air, while howling at the top of his lungs!

He began to grunt and jump up and down like a crazed beast! He was snorting angrily, while his red eyes glowed! His huge gross tongue began to flick against his dreadful fang-like teeth!

"Run!!!" I screamed.

Nathan and I instinctively grabbed Sissy's hands, and the three of us quickly ran to the other side of the cave! There was no way we could climb up – it was a frozen sheet of ice! We would slip right back down!

We had no choice. We knew we were going to have to run back into the cave!

We headed back in, slipping and sliding on the ice. There was another tunnel! Abominable was now growling and chasing us, while the cave shook from his pounding steps! We were dodging icicles that were falling from the ceiling!

"Over here !" I said.

We turned a corner, and quickly ducked behind some ice formations. We sat silently, hoping the horrible beast would go the other way.

But he didn't! I looked over at Sissy and saw a tear roll down her cheek from being so completely terrified.

She looked at me while quickly wiping it away and shook her head "no," as if to say, "it was over for us."

Then I saw Nathan squeeze her hand, and I knew how much they liked each other. It was at that moment, I knew if we made it out of this mess alive, I would be happy for my best friend and cousin and not act so selfish anymore...

The cave was filled with the heavy grunt-like breathing of the beast. I knew he was close by, I peeked out to see where he was – hoping that he had gone past us.

When I saw he was directly in front of us, I was so shocked, I lost my balance on the ice! Within seconds, I was sliding straight for the vicious Abominable Snowman!!!

Chapter Seven - Scary

"HEEEELLLLLPPPP!!!" I screamed, while trying to stop myself from sliding!

"NOOOO!" Nathan yelled.

I was trying everything I could to stop slipping toward him, but I was heading right into the Abominable's giant feet. He was bending over, getting ready to grab me!

Suddenly it was crazy! Nathan and Sissy were scrambling to save me. They were trying to distract the beast!

We were all slipping and sliding on the ice. The beast was so confused watching us, I had a split second to get on my hands and knees and crawl away. But just as I did, I felt claws sinking into my leg!

"Sissy, grab an icicle!" I heard Nathan yell.

They pulled giant icicles from the ceiling and were pounding on Abominable with them!

When Abominable turned to whack them, I managed to get away! I quickly grabbed an icicle and rammed it into the beast's side. He spun around with all his might, his giant claws coming my way, I ducked, and he fell from the spin!

"C'mon!" I yelled.

There was no time. We had seconds to get away, while Abominable laid there dazed. It wouldn't be long until the beast came out of it, and this time, it would really be enraged!

We couldn't go back out of the cave the same way we came in, because we would have to go past Abominable. Besides, there was no way we could climb up that steep ice. We would either be caught, or fall into the freezing water! And if we were caught we would end up becoming one of the beast's icy human popsicles for sure!

"This way," said Nathan.

There were three long tunnels to choose from; one was the icy slide that got us into this mess, the other tunnel was totally dark, but the third had light blue ice.

"There has to be an opening somewhere, because of the light reflection!"

At that moment, I was so thankful that my best friend liked science.

By now we could hear the beast roaring, it was madder than ever!

We began running as fast as we could! This side of the massive cave didn't seem as frozen, and some of the ground was slushy, making it easier to run on.

The thuds began again, now the beast was coming up on us fast! It was almost like he could smell us. He probably could…he was an animal. Fortunately, the cave seemed to be getting lighter, thanks to the reflection of the blue ice.

It had now narrowed to a passageway, getting smaller and smaller and tapering off. It seemed like we were starting to run upwards.

"We are going to be trapped in here," cried Sissy.

"Don't stop! He'll catch us." I said.

"There has to be a way out," declared Nathan.

It was getting steep, almost like we were starting to crawl up a rising slope of ice steps.

We could hear the pounding footsteps – Abominable was gaining on us!

Chapter Eight - Scary

Time was running out!

"Look! Up ahead! What's that?" I asked, as I pointed to a glint of light. It was coming in from a slit in the side of the cave wall.

"It looks like a small opening!" yelled Sissy.

We continued up the slanted path as it became more and more of an incline and harder to climb.

When we got to the opening, light was shining through two small slits on either side of a massive ice block.

"Let's see if we can move this!" I stated.

With all of our might, we began to try to push the frozen wall.

"Here, try from this side!" said Nathan.

Again, we put all of our strength into it, but it was no use. The frozen block would only move a fraction of an inch, then slip back into place.

"He's getting closer!" whispered Sissy frantically.

She was right! The slanted steps we were on – began to shake!

"Push harder!" I panicked.

But it was no use…we could hear the fearsome Abominable heading up the icy slope directly toward us!

I quickly glanced around and then headed up a couple steps, it got even steeper as it curved sharply to the left.

"We might have a chance," I whispered, carefully coming back down.

"Sissy, give me your scarf!"

"What? I'm freezing as it is," she said.

"Just do it!" I barked.

Sissy quickly took off her scarf and handed it to me.

"Nathan, you and Sissy push on the block with all of your might when I say go," I explained.

"Go!"

As they pushed the frozen block, it gave me just enough space to smash Sissy's scarf into the thin opening.

"C'mon!" I whispered, as they followed me further up the curving slope to hide around the corner.

Nathan and Sissy knew what I was up to.

Abominable, like any creature, probably used it's sense of smell. Since Sissy's scarf had her girly perfume all over it, hopefully, he would think we moved the block and escaped through the opening with Sissy's scarf getting caught and left behind.

We held our breath…he was just feet away; if this didn't work, we would be the Abominable Snowman's dinner!

Chapter Nine - Scary

The Abominable almost stomped right past Sissy's scarf – then he stopped.

His enormous head turned, as icky gooey snot flew out of his gross looking nose onto his dingy white fur. He would grind his gigantic, sharp teeth together, while looking around.

He stared at the scarf. He was going to go for it…but, no! He began to turn away. It was almost as if he sensed we were nearby.

He began to move up the slanted ice, then stopped for a second and let out a ferocious growl! He turned back to the scarf, violently yanked it out of the small gap and began to eat it! He chewed on it like a maniac!

In one swift move his massive hands picked up the huge icy block and moved it aside. He busted out of the cave on a rampage, looking for us.

"We have to get out of here while we can," I whispered, my voice shaking.

"Yeah, but what if he's right out there?" asked Sissy.

"We…we…we…have a better chance out there, than in…in here," said Nathan, choking out the words.

110

We carefully began to approach the opening, when suddenly, there was thunderous growling and snarling! We stopped motionless in our tracks, listening.

This time it wasn't the same sounds that the Abominable made. It sounded almost like a lion, but much louder and angrier! Maybe more like a bear.

We edged our way forward to see what was going on as the sounds grew louder. Sure enough! It was a gigantic polar bear…almost half the size of Abominable – but still pretty huge! It had to weigh at least 1000 lbs!

It was standing on its hind legs and roaring. Abominable was directly across from it, howling. The vicious beasts would swat at the air, as they circled each other!

The site of their open mouths with vicious sharp teeth as they snarled and growled at each other was terrifying! It was going to be a gruesome fight, one that we didn't want to stay around to watch!

We knew if they saw us, they would forget about fighting and come after us! Not knowing what to do, we waited a few seconds until they were just about to battle… then it started.

Abominable moved in and knocked the polar bear to the ground…but not for long! The polar bear chomped down on Abominable's arm, and immediately its matted fur began to turn a bright red!

We knew we couldn't watch this ghastly scene any longer; we had to get out of there. I signaled to Nathan to move forward, but to stay as close to the wall as he could. We slowly and quietly made our way out into the cold fresh air.

By now, the beasts were rolling and tumbling as they struggled in a ghastly fight! Fur was flying everywhere, and there were puddles of blood on the ice! When we were almost around the side of the cave, they began to roll our way!

"Look out!" yelled Sissy.

It alerted the scary beasts! They stopped fighting and turned their massive heads our way! They began growling and started to come after us! But as they did, both of them began to slip in the disgusting puddles and started to slide down the ravine! Within seconds, they were falling fast!

Moments later, they both splashed into the freezing, cold bay water. Abominable grabbed onto the icy shoreline and climbed up onto a piece of ice, but his weight caused it to break away. The polar bear quickly swam to shore, climbed up, and sat licking his wounds.

Abominable looked frantic as it tried to get back to shore on the ice float, but the current was too strong as he drifted out toward the wide open sea!

There was no way we were going to wait and see what happened. Nathan pulled out his compass, found the direction that we needed to go, and we took off running. This time avoiding any holes that might be hidden before us.

Even though we were frozen, cold, and tired, we were moving quickly. There was not a chance we were going to slow down, just in case any ferocious beast started chasing us.

We were so lucky to be alive!

Chapter Eleven - Scary

Four Months Later...

School was a few weeks away from getting out for the summer, which was pretty exciting. Being a kid, summer was the best time of year, for me, anyway. Especially since, I really lost my liking of snow after our terrifying experience in Alaska.

Sometimes, I would wake up with nightmares about the Abominable Snowman...especially since I knew it was NO myth!

So, when I got home from school, it was kind of weird to find Mom and Dad glued to the television. Not only did they never-ever watch TV during the day, they were usually at the station. But today, they were actually watching a live news show. And it was about the finding of an Abominable Snowman floating off the coast of Russia in a frozen ice block!

"Mick, can you believe it?" Mom asked.

I swallowed hard, the sight of seeing this preserved frozen beast again sent shivers up and down my spine!

I stood in silence, staring at the story on TV.

"Man, I wish we could've discovered that beast while filming there! Don't you Mick?" Dad exclaimed. "Look at the size of him!"

"Uhh…yeah…jeez," was all that I could manage to say, as I stood in shock, watching the show.

"That would've done wonders for the stations ratings," said Mom.

All I could think about was calling Nathan and Sissy to see if they knew about the vicious creature being found.

The show did a close up of the gory, ferocious Abominables face. How we got away from that beast, I'll never know.

"Oh, and by the way, I know you'll be excited about this," continued Mom. "We just got our instructions for the next Uncover Station's Myth Solver Show, and this summer we are going to…

All I heard was "…next Uncover Station's Myth Solver Show," as I continued to stare at the wicked beast on TV.

But then I thought, *what could possibly be worse?*

Little did I know I would soon find out!

The End

We decided we should go back to town to do some investigating. The wilderness seemed too icy and frozen for us to go alone.

We would see if we could borrow a snowmobile to make our lives a little easier, instead of trying to trudge through mounds of snow and ice-covered glaciers.

"You know, Nathan, I would love to try out my snowboard," I stated, as we began walking.

"Oh yeah…like they are sooo sweet – these babies just fly!" answered Nathan enthusiastically.

"You guys and your crazy sports," yawned Sissy. "If that is what you two are going to do, then I am going to go back to the hotel to take a nap!"

Nathan and I looked at each other, smiling widely, while nodding.

"Fine! I don't care…just wake me when you want to play grown-up myth solvers!" mocked Sissy.

"Ha, ha, ha…Grown-up?!" I began to laugh. "Do you have any idea the kind of people that are into snowboarding? It's not just for kids, ya know! Extreme sports are major!"

"Totally!" agreed Nathan, making Sissy even angrier.

117

"Well, like, none of the people I hang around with do it, so, whatever!" she huffed.

We were nearing Main Street, and Sissy took off ahead of us. We stood watching her stomp up the steps to the hotel. When she got to the top, she was so irritated she looked at us, turned one shoulder our way and made a face, then stormed into the hotel.

"Girls!" I stated.

"Maybe we should include her," said Nathan sheepishly.

"Are you kidding? We'd spend the entire time teaching her how to board. Besides, she would probably want to ride it downhill like a sled!"

We laughed and quickly made our way to one of the hills for snowboarding.

Some of the boarders were unbelievable! We watched as they shredded the slopes. We were amazed!

It wasn't long before we were recognized because of the "Myth Solver Show" hat I was wearing; and we introduced ourselves to some of the locals.

With a little guidance from them, we began to try out our snowboarding skills! Our boards were unbelievable, but our skills weren't.

We had a great time boarding, and when it became dusk, we figured we better head back to the hotel.

We got back just in time, as the crew and our parents were pulling in from a long day of filming.

"Hey!" said Mom, jumping out of the RV.

"Hi, Mom! Hi, Dad! We're starved!" I said, knowing, at that instant, my mom would have something to say about my greeting…but, at that exact moment, an angry Sissy stomped out of the hotel and yelled, "Ohhhh…nice, like, everybody show up together, leaving me here alone all day!"

I couldn't have been luckier. Her grand entrance made my "Hello, I'm hungry" seem like I was rolling out the red carpet – compared to her rude welcome.

Uncle Hayden stormed up the steps of the hotel and ushered Sissy in by the arm. I was snickering to myself, until I caught Nathan giving me a dirty look.

Once inside the hotel, we had a fantastic dinner. Lots of Alaskan fare, like fish, some seafood, fish, and, oh yeah, more fish! But everything was delicious, and we were stuffed.

We thought we were finished, until they brought out dessert and what could it be? But Baked Alaska! We laughed at the name; Alaska was anything but warm and baked. But we found room for the yummy cake that was covered with ice cream and a fluffy sweet coating – delish!

It had been a great day! It was so much fun, I had almost forgot about myth solving, until our parents and the crew began to chat about the pretty worthless day of filming crazy Atka.

Nathan, Sissy, and I laughed at the ridiculous stories they told about her. They were sure that Atka had made up most of her wild tales, especially the ones about Abominable coming with the "magic sky."

We had no idea that in only a matter of hours – we would see how real Atka's stories were.

Nathan and I already decided we were going to do a little Myth Solving later on. We knew we would have to sneak out of our rooms when everyone went to sleep.

Later that night, when I was sure that everyone was asleep, I quietly climbed out of bed. I quickly took my pajamas off, which I had put on over my clothes to fool my mom when she came in to check on me.

This time, I made sure that I had on enough warm gear, including extra socks and long underwear. If it was that cold during the day, I couldn't imagine how cold it would be at night!

I put on my backpack and very quietly snuck out of my room and tiptoed to Nathan's door. I did one knock on the door.

He carefully opened it and came out ready to go. We did our secret handshake and began to sneak down the hall.

"Eh-hem!" we heard from behind us.

We froze in our footsteps! I was sure our parents caught us! We slowly turned around to see a giant, pink puff ball standing with her hands on her hips, staring at us.

She walked up to us and whispered directly in our faces, "Like, don't even say a word!"

This time, she was fuming. We should've included her, now we would have to be super, super nice to her.

We walked out of the hotel, and it felt magical outside! The sky was dark blue with millions of twinkling white lights…there were a zillion stars, plus, it was a full moon.

It was 10:30PM, and we heard that we might be able to see the Northern Lights that night.

We headed around to the side of the hotel. There was the snowmobile the front desk clerk said we could borrow. Luckily, it was a big machine with enough room for the three of us. The key was tucked under the helmet, just like he said it would be.

We jumped on. I had experience on one of these vehicles at the producer's cottage up north, so I gave everyone the safety speech.

I turned the key and revved up the snowmobile.

"Helmets on?" I asked.

"Helmet's on!" Sissy and Nathan replied.

"Okay…hold on tight!"

We sped off under the glistening sky. We weren't even thinking about the danger that would soon be in our path.

As we were gliding along, we were kind of inspecting the area. Every once in awhile we would stop and hop off, checking for any Abominable footprints…when the sky suddenly began to glow! It was the most mystical, magical thing I have ever seen. It was beautiful arcs of dancing green florescent ribbons going up to the dark night sky!

"It's the Aurora Borealis!" said Nathan excitedly. "Also, said to be sunlight reflecting off polar snow and ice."

It was so amazing, it even made Sissy forget she was mad at us.

"That's just awesome!" she exclaimed. "But it reminds me of something I've seen recently, and I just can't seem to put my finger on it."

"Yeah, me, too," stated Nathan curiously.

We got back on the snowmobile and continued down the deserted street for awhile. We passed Atka's neighborhood, and we were now in an abandoned area, cruising past some old empty buildings. We were enjoying the breathtaking magical sky – when all of a sudden there was something up ahead on the path.

"Look!" I yelled, while trying to shine the snowmobile light on it.

"Maybe it's someone that needs help," said Sissy.

"Out here?" I questioned.

Seconds later it vanished!

"I think we should head back to the hotel," said Nathan.

We agreed, but seconds later, a massive creature jumped out at us! It just missed us by inches!

It was a giant beast covered with white fur from head to toe, and it was huge! It had a massive head with glowing, white fang-like teeth! Its long claws scraped against the windshield as we flew by!

"It's Abominable!" I screamed. "Hold on!" I did a complete turn with the snowmobile while gunning it and trying to get away from the beast!

Sissy and Nathan were holding on as tight as they could as I pushed the machine up to 80 miles an hour – but the freakiest thing was, *the beast was keeping up with us!*

"Here we go!" I yelled, as we flew over a snowbank and began heading toward some of the abandoned buildings!

They were ancient, rundown wooden buildings with peeling paint. There was one giant structure in the middle. It almost looked like a snow covered ghost town – but it was some kind of abandoned factory.

We flew in-between the broken down buildings, we were going so fast and turning so quickly, we were starting to lose Abominable!

We knew we were going to have to ditch the snowmobile if we wanted to stay alive! We pulled into an alleyway and hid the snowmobile behind some old, giant metal barrels next to the largest building.

"What are you doing? We can't stop, we have to get away!" whispered Sissy in a panic.

"We can't out run him on this! I have a plan."

"Trust your cousin, Sissy!" insisted Nathan.

The giant door was locked, so we quickly snuck around to the side, and, once we were sure the coast was clear, we ran and hid behind a broken down wall.

We didn't hear or see Abominable anywhere. Little did we know, he had already found us!

It was frightfully quiet. We cowered, motionless, behind the wall, as we stared at the brilliant Northern Lights dancing in the sky.

The stillness of the abandoned factory in the middle of nowhere and the snow glistening green from the color of the sky, made us almost forget about our horrifying situation.

"Hey! I got it!" whispered Sissy.

"Great! Got what?" I asked.

"That amulet Atka gave you…"

"I was really hoping you had a plan to save us, but what about it?" I asked, as I pulled it out of my jacket.

"It matches the Northern Lights!" exclaimed Sissy. "Look, hold it up."

"Yeah…It does," I said, as I held the amulet up to the sky…The minute I did, there was a brilliant flash.

We were blinded by the light for a few seconds.

"Wow, what was that?" asked Nathan.

We rubbed our eyes, and when we opened them, we were all standing behind an enormous wall!

"Whaaaa….? How did we get here?" asked Nathan, looking around.

126

"I don't know," I replied.

"Something is totally weird," said Sissy.

"Uhhhh…I think we shrunk!" stated Nathan.

"That is very funny!" I laughed.

"No, look around. I'm serious, I think we're tiny!" he exclaimed.

We looked over ourselves, at our clothes, our shoes; we seemed to look exactly the same…

"Mick, the minute you held that amulet up to the sky, there was that shocking bright light and POOF! It's a spell! It's cuz of that necklace!" insisted Sissy.

"You guys are right! Look, the buildings are huge now."

We turned to look. The deserted buildings were ten times bigger!

Now we were really in trouble! At that exact moment, Abominable came running around the corner of a building, growling ferociously!

We froze, then realized he didn't see us! He was huffing and puffing and snorting and standing directly in front of us! The problem was, from where we were, he had grown a few thousand feet bigger!

We watched, motionless, as he turned his head quickly back and forth. Then he scratched his head and continued looking around for us! The beast was confused!

We knew the only way we were going to see if we had really shrunk was to get to the snowmobile...which could be a real problem!

Things were really strange. We could walk on top of the snow, but we had to be careful to avoid any of Abominable's massive footprints, so we wouldn't fall into the large open holes.

We moved to the alleyway where we had hidden the snowmobile. It seemed like a much farther walk than the few feet it was before.

When we finally got around the massive metal barrels, we were shocked to see the snowmobile had become gigantic!

There was no way we could ride it. I could see that the key was probably the same size as we were!

128

We were shrunk and stranded, and Abominable was hunting for us!

"Look – over there!" I shouted.

It was a small, curved opening straight ahead of us leading into the huge deserted building.

"C'mon, Abominable can't fit through that!" yelled Sissy.

We ran to the small opening.

"Well, this is a weird little round archway," I said, as we trudged though it.

Once inside, there was a strange eerie feeling to the place, and it had a wicked odor. It was some kind of enormous, cold, dark, deserted factory. Fortunately, the light from outside was streaming in through the broken windows. There were holes in the old tin roof – rusted and falling in.

The sky made the walls look a dingy, grey-green color, and the cement floor was littered with garbage and frozen puddles. There were metal pieces lying on old dilapidated assembly lines.

Everywhere we looked, there were old tin cans. Some smashed in gigantic piles, some still in one piece, and most of them lying around, rusted out. There were old barrels overflowing with rotting fish bones.

"I think it's an old cannery," said Nathan.

"Ouuu… it stinks!" added Sissy, as she covered her nose.

What we didn't know was, one of those stinky old cans would save our lives!

We were so busy looking around the massive disgusting place, we hadn't noticed the scratching coming from behind us. When we turned to look, we were freaked out by a giant gross rat that was heading directly for us!

We took off running as fast as we could! But the giant beast, and its sharp teeth with saggy white whiskers, was looking for something to eat, and we were it!

"This way!" yelled Sissy, as we headed toward the massive canning area. "Look, over there! That giant screw driver! Hurry, get it!"

We ran to the screwdriver with the rat chasing after us.

"On the count of three…" I instructed, and we all lifted the heavy screwdriver.

"What? Is he tired of fish bones for dinner?" asked Nathan sarcastically. It was kind of funny how, in these tight situations, Nathan's humor would always come out. I always enjoyed it, except now I didn't have time to laugh!

We picked up the heavy screwdriver, and when the vicious rat got too close to us, we would jab at it! We would almost hit it... just missing it every time!

The rat would circle around us, with foam coming out of its mouth while its buck teeth would move up and down. Its repulsive tail would swing around at the same time, just missing us!

We would have to co-ordinate turning with each other.

"Go left, go left!" Nathan yelled.

"This is getting too heavy...I don't know how long I can hold it!" hollered Sissy.

"I know...to your right!" I yelled. "See that net over there?"

"Watch out!" screamed Nathan, as the rat tried to lunge at us!

We hit it and cut its nose, and now it was really mad!

"...the net!" I continued.

"Yeah!" Sissy and Nathan hollered back.

"When I say, 'Go!', with all our might, let's try to throw the screwdriver at the rat and then run to the net!" I bellowed.

"On your mark, get set, go!"

We threw the screwdriver at the rat! Then ran as fast as we could to the giant net; it was apparently an old fishing net, and we began to climb up it. We managed to get high-enough where the disgusting rat couldn't get us!

"Whew!" I said, suspended in mid-air, while clinging to the net!

The rat paced below us and, every once in awhile, would stand on his hind legs sniffing with its bloody nose while looking at us.

The situation was so bad, we didn't know what to do. When we would try to climb higher, the rat would chew on the net, causing it shake so much, we would have to hang on as tightly as we could....Not only that, we would have to dodge tin cans rolling down at us from the top of the table the net was on!

It would only be a matter of seconds, before we would be in an even more dangerous spot!

The sound of wood cracking filled the air, like a door being busted through. Thuds began to shake the deserted cannery, cans began rolling everywhere!

There it was, a huge looming shadow, and it was heading our way!

"Climb!" I yelled, but now Abominable was only a few feet away from us!

The disgusting rat continued to pull and gnaw on the net!

We didn't know if Abominable could see us or not, but we knew he could see the rat – because he was sneaking right up behind it!

In one quick swoop, he picked up the rat! But the rat still had the net in its mouth! *We were being pulled with the rat and the net!*

Seconds later, the Abominable Snowman did the most disgusting thing that we had ever seen – he started to eat the rat!

"Don't look!" I whispered, as he finished putting the whole thing in his mouth. "Get to the top!" Now we were crawling across the net toward the cans. It was almost too unbelievable…like we were on some kind of crazy reality show!

We made it to the top of the table just in time, but as we were about to hide behind some cans, we froze!

Abominables mammoth face leaned in, he saw us!

He was inches away, staring right at us with his eyes wide open! He was breathing so heavily, he was almost knocking us over, that, and his awful smelling breath!

He slowly lifted one of his humongous arms, moving his huge hand toward me! He was about to flick me with his claw – "Hide!" Nathan yelled.

"GGGGRRRRRRRR!" Abominable grunted, as we moved behind a can!

With one quick flick, he knocked some of the cans down to the floor.

We ran and hid behind others, but the beast was now snorting loudly while moving the cans and looking for us. We were moving can to can. It was almost like this beast was enjoying this – like it was some kind of game to him!

"I've got and idea," I whispered.

One of the cans was lying on its side, right near the net, but far enough away from the beast. We carefully snuck to it and climbed in. We knew what we had to do now.

At the very next moment, when the beast knocked more of them over – we began to push from inside the can.

135

When we got it rolling, we started running with the can. It was like we were hamsters in one of those giant clear balls – only it was a tin can!

It was a crazy ride, rolling down the net and then thumping to the floor. The Abominable had no clue we had escaped...until he knocked the few last cans off the table!

All of the cans stopped rolling, except ours, as we
continued running inside of it as fast as we could! Within a
few seconds, we knew that the beast had noticed, because we
could hear the thuds coming our way.

Seconds later, our can came to an abrupt stop. We
could no longer run and make it move!

"Hang on!" I said terrified. "This could get ugly!"

In the next few moments it felt like we were on some
kind of crazy amusement park ride. The can suddenly went
upright, and we all fell on top of each other. As we struggled
to get our bearings, the beast was peering in at us! He then
began to hold it above his head!

The most terrifying thing of all happened! He turned
the can upside down while looking at us! There wasn't
anything to hold on too! We started to fall from what
seemed like thousands of feet up in the air!

Luckily, we were right above the horrendous beast's
head! We fell right onto the middle of his FACE! For a
second we were in shock, we just looked at each other
scattered about on this giant fur-ball!

But there was no time to waste! His huge hands were coming at us as he looked cross-eyed! He was going to squish us like bugs!

"Now what?" cried Sissy, as she tried to stand up, while completely grossed out by being tangled in his dirty fur!

"Do anything you can to avoid thooosseee giaannnt hannnddddsss!" I yelled, as I ran toward her and pushed her down, just missing his hand.

"Try to make him dizzy!" hollered Nathan.

"Yeah, maybe if we irritate him, we can get to his back and run down him...but hold on!" I screamed, while pulling on his fur as hard as I could. I made my way up to the top of his head.

I looked over, and Sissy had moved to his nose and was pinching it!

Nathan was at his eye kicking it, and I went for its ear, punching and yelling into it.

We would move to another spot while making our way up…he was getting so irritated. He kept trying to catch us, and, pretty soon, we had the beast spinning in circles! It seemed like he was starting to stumble from being so dizzy!

"You better hold on!" screamed Nathan. "He's getting dizzy!"

Nathan was right, the beast was woozy! When he would try to hit us, his arm would just flail around in the air! We kept pounding on him and agitating him more and more.

Nathan and I moved to the middle of his head, while burrowing into his fur.

"Move over here!" I instructed Sissy.

She tried to make her way over, but the beast was so dizzy he began to slip! We were holding on with all our might as I watched Sissy, but it looked like it was too late! As the beast dropped to the ground, we could no longer see Sissy!

He hit the ground hard! He was out cold!

We began to call out for Sissy, and, thankfully, a few seconds later, she popped her head up from inside his ear.

"I just tied one of his ear hairs around my waist! It was totally gross – but it saved my life!" she laughed.

The cannery had grown dark as we swiftly made our way off of Abominable, knowing that there was no time to spare, and he could wake up at any moment!

Once we were on the floor, Nathan and I grabbed our flashlights out of our backpacks. They didn't do much in the cavernous place, they were too tiny, but they were good enough to help us find our way back to the rat door and outside!

We knew there was no time to spare, just in case any more rats were lurking around, or Abominable woke up.

In the darkness outside, we realized there was one major, or tiny problem – we didn't have any way to get back to the hotel! We were still too small and shrunken!

Seconds later, a sliver of the dawn's sunlight lit up the sky…my amulet was still hanging outside of my jacket as the tiny beam of light seemed to shoot right at it. Again, an enormous burst of light blinded us, and we all fell backwards.

"I just can't take this anymore. I want to be my own size, and I want to get back to the hotel!" Sissy cried, rubbing her eyes.

"Me, too. I don't know what to do now." I stated, as I stood up and started to walk over to the snowmobile.

"I wish I could figure out a way we could ride this thing back," I said sadly.

"Why don't you just get on it?" asked Nathan, laughing.

"I wish, I cou…" I looked at the snowmobile and realized that I could get on it!

I was back to normal size!

Nathan and Sissy were too! They jumped up, ran over, and we all laughed and hugged!

"One second!" I said.

"What are you doing?" asked Nathan, as I headed for the door to the cannery where we had left Abominable.

I snapped the amulet off my neck, stepped in the door that Abominable had broken down and threw the amulet at the knocked-out Abominable.

It landed right on top of him! I walked back out to a very happy Sissy and Nathan.

"Well, jump on, and let's get back before everyone wakes up!" I said, smiling.

We quickly put on our helmets.

"Hold on!" I yelled, as we sped off on the snow covered road in a glorious Alaskan sunrise.

The Full Size Ending

The End

It was one myth solving trip that I would never forget!

Needless to say, I was happy to see that everyone was doing fine and living together peacefully.

It was great to see the Abominable Snowman was doing so well.

Now, I kept up with what was happening by writing to Atka and reading the Skagway news online.

Whoever would have thought that a beast like that, which was a myth for so many hundreds of years, would be able to co-exist with humans?

Maybe that was what it was trying to do all along, but people were always so afraid of the mythical beast.

He was already doing sign language and had never shown any type of anger, except when Atka would leave from visiting him.

Abominable proved to be more human than any kind of animal.

We had been on every news show there was after capturing Abominable, and Atka was an international celebrity.

It had been a month since we had gotten back from Alaska. I was back in school and trying to downplay the celebrity thing…it had gotten kind of annoying.

Reverse - Eight Chapter

Our jobs, as myth solvers for this mission, were over. This was one of the most important missions we had ever done. The terrific crew had caught everything on tape.

Now that the Abominable was captured, and Atka was safe, there was nothing that could be done except to bring him in.

The cage was transported hanging from a helicopter.

They had put him in a gigantic cage – the same kind of cages they used for polar bears when they were captured in the wild.

Then they hooked the straps onto the helicopter and lifted him into the cage. He weighed so much, they had to put giant leather straps with big metal clasps around him.

It was the actual living Myth! Although peacefully sleeping at the moment. We immediately gathered around to help as we looked in astonishment at the Abominable Snowman!

"I guarantee we won't hurt him," said one of the police officers.

"He good beast. No hurt, no hurt! I fine, I fine!" yelled Atka.

"I'm so glad you're all right!" said Mom while she hugged Atka.

Atka seemed completely unafraid and calm.

We ran into the cave!

Reverse - Seven Chapter

The giant beast immediately fell backwards with a heavy thud.

They got him! We held our breath...*Boom!*

James had the camera rolling.

They steadied the gun...

The police officer, along with a local veterinarian, grabbed a giant tranquilizer gun.

She was tied up. We gave her the sign to be quiet and not let on that she could see us.

By chance, the beast had his back to us. He was trying to communicate with her! Every once in awhile he would grunt at her! The enormous Abominable was sitting directly across from Atka just staring at her.

He had long white fur and a massive head! It was the Abominable Snowman! He was huge!

Reverse - Six Chapter

There they were! It was a sight like something we had never seen in our lives…and probably never will again.

We slowly and cautiously crept up to the cave.

The helicopter would have to circle a good distance from the site, and the snowmobiles and the dogsled would have to stay back, too. We knew we couldn't startle him with any loud noises if they were in the cave.

The search was over. Before long, we could see a cave in the distance, not too far from Atka's house. The beast didn't know it had made it super easy for us to track it.

It could obviously move extremely fast and was very agile and good at hiding.

We got lucky, it would make the search a lot easier following these giant footprints! It had to be Abominable! There were massive footprints in the snow! We weren't on the trail long, and we stopped in shock!

The crew, our parents, and some of the police were on snowmobiles. It was a major search party with a helicopter, too, and us on the dog sled.

The police looked around, knowing that we had no time to waste. Probably the best way to track her would be to take her dogs and the dogsled!

Within 10 minutes, the police, along with a helicopter unit and snowmobiles, were on Atka's property. He told them that this time it was really serious.

"We have to notify the police!" said Dad, as he quickly began to punch in 911 for emergencies.

Reverse – Five Chapter

Something had really upset these dogs. One of her dogs had even tried to dig out of the pen. We gave them some treats to calm them down, it helped, but they continued whimpering. We went outside to check on her dogs, they were growling and going crazy.

"To think that we didn't believe her, we thought that she was just a crazy person!" I stated.

We continued looking around, but it was clear she had vanished.

We carefully looked in every closet. It was obvious there had been a struggle. Stuff was everywhere.

"Atka! Aaaattttkkkkkaaa! Aaattkkkaa!" everyone began to call her.

"Maybe we should call out her name, what if she's afraid and just hiding somewhere?" questioned Sissy.

We moved inside the house, cautiously – our parents and the crew had stun guns, just in case a beast really had broken in. We got out of the trucks.

The house looked worse than it did the first time we had seen it. This time the front door was completely off its hinges. The path was strewn with torn up brush and trees. We could hear her dogs howling and barking in the back.

Reverse - Four Chapter

But something was wrong, really wrong…

We thought for sure we would find her ready for her second taping, probably sitting in her kitchen, drinking green tea.

We pulled down the road to her house and, unlike the normally brightly lit home, it appeared to be dark.

We drove down the winding road toward Atka's home, and, every once in awhile, I would take a break from my game to take in the breathtaking views of Alaska. Even though it wasn't a long drive, the road was winding and lined with trees and glacier views.

Occasionally, someone would yell, "Moose!", and we would see one of those amazing animals in clear view.

Nathan and I ignored her.

"I'm tired and bored. I don't have one of those game thingy's," moaned Sissy, as she plopped down on one of the bunks.

Nathan and I continued gaming.

"Okay, Mom. We will," I replied.

"It's really not polite to ignore Sissy, and it would be great if you two actually talked to each other instead of gaming, especially when you are right in front of each other," insisted Mom.

Even though it was a rented RV, it was pretty nice, but not as nice as the Myth Mobile.

The crew jumped into the trucks, and we loaded into the RV. Ready for another exciting day of Myth Solving and trying to figure out Atka.

We thanked her, as she warned us to "stay warm and be careful."

As we left the hotel, the owner's wife ran out to give us a basket of home baked muffins, even though we were stuffed from breakfast.

The next morning we packed up our gear and headed down to breakfast. I noticed that Sissy inched her way in, trying to sit next to Nathan, and all I could think of was *yuk*!

Reverse - Three Chapter

We had no clue that Atka knew what was coming…

We were headed back to the hotel, and we waved goodbye as we pulled down the road.

"Maybe she's expecting a big snow storm or high winds tonight or something," stated Uncle Hayden, as he turned our rented RV around in the driveway, "You know this place is known for heavy wind."

When we left, she strangely began to bolt and lock all her windows, even her outside shutters.

"Atka stay in her home" she insisted.

But she violently shook her head, "no." They told her that we had to go, and she was welcome to come with us.

One of the crew members went and got her a drink of water, while Mom and Dad tried to talk to her. Eventually, they calmed her down.

As she threw herself to the ground, she began yelling, "He come for me! He come for meeeeee!"

Suddenly, she began to scream and wave her hands in the air. It was totally weird!

We explained that we would see her in the morning as we said our goodbyes. She knew spells and chants and believed in mysterious things. Atka was a native from another small village on the far side of Alaska, and she had turned out to be really interesting.

Reverse – Two Chapter

Until it came time to leave Atka...

Nothing had really happened. It was a pretty lousy day when it came to myth solving.

The crew began to wrap up and put away the equipment, they said they got some crazy stories from Atka, but not much else. Tomorrow, they would plan on getting some outside shots around her house.

It seemed like we were only gone an hour or so, but apparently it was longer, and we made it back just in time.

It was a riot! We were laughing so hard…we felt like we were in the Iditarod – the famous dogsled race!

Before we knew it, we were flying!

We didn't want to go too fast and were careful to stay on the main trail. We had headed out into the trails with the dogsled, it was totally cool.

It seemed pretty easy, as she showed us how to hook it up. She said we could use the dogsled, but warned us not to go too far. Her mysterious black eyes looked troubled. It was clear that she really loved her dogs.

Atka came out with some treats for us to give them.

She had six of them, and they were a mix of Siberian Huskies and Alaskan Malamutes. Her beautiful dogs were in a pen in the back.

There was so much snow on the ground, and it was really cold and windy. So, I was glad that we were bundled up, even if we did look like walking marshmallows. Mom always worried about me getting too cold.

We decided to go around to the back of Atka's house.

Reverse – Chapter One

NATIONAL SCAR NEWS

The Tabloid Ending

STUNNING END TO THE SNOWMAN SEARCH!

LUNCH LADY KNOCKED UNCONSCIOUS AFTER STUDENT'S GASSY ATTACK OF CAFETERIA BEANS

The Abominable Family Reveals Itself and Joins Civilization!

It was a sight to be seen on the quiet, chilly streets of Skagway, Alaska yesterday Saturday, February 12Th at about 10:00AM, Alaska Time; when four Abominable Snowpeople made their way into the small town! They pulled in on their dogsled, parked it and attempted to make their way into the local diner.

As they approached the area, word spread faster than a teenager texting as horror filled the streets. After these beasts had lived shrouded in mystery for hundreds of years, hunted and blamed for strange happenings, to see them in the small town of Skagway drew utter shock and fear!

Luckily, the Myth Solver film crew from the Uncover Network was in town, and was notified immediately. They had quickly set up their gear to capture the entire event live; while police, state troopers, and the fire department, along with a few brave townspeople quickly lined the streets to protect the town.

The largest of the four Abominable weighing about 700 pounds and standing about eight feet tall, slowly disembarked the dogsled. He held his hands up in the air – as if to signal we mean you no harm. The mood was nervous and silent, except for the tightening of the grips on the weapons the locals held, and then the unthinkable happened!

In plain and clear English, the large furry beast said, "How dee-doo neighbors?"

A sense of relief filled the streets! Immediately following his greeting the second largest Abominable climbed out of the sled, and in a females voice (she had curly fur on top of her head) said, "We would like to move to Skagway and live among friends!"

Cheers filled the air! Immediately real estate sales people and bankers broke through the police barriers and began rushing toward the Abominables!

Shocked, and in fear with all the commotion they caused, the gi-nourmous Abominables quickly pulled their children into a huddle.

Immediately the police stepped in and cleared the way for the Myth Solver team to interview the Abominables. The host's of the show cautiously approached them with microphones.

"May we ask you a few questions?" asked the overjoyed hosts.

"Yeah, as long as these folk don't mind if we have breakfast first, that is, before we look at any homes." answered the large male Abominable timidly, and then he laughed an extremely loud and ferocious laugh. Immediately, the other Abominables joined in laughing. This caused instant panic as people covered their ears, while the heavy laughter practically blew the bystanders hair back.

Within seconds, the laughter had spread through the entire crowd; people began laughing and circling around the giant snow creatures. White fur was flying everywhere while they shook hands and were escorted into the diner.

The restaurant was packed, people shouted questions, and reporters struggled to listen to the Myth Solvers interview the Abominable family. Throughout the day, reporters began to flood into Skagway from all parts of the world. Helicopters were descending everywhere, and the diner quickly ran out of food, including the Abominable family's favorite dish of Vanilla ice cream with pancakes and sardines.

Mick Morris, his friend Nathan, and Cousin Sissy were seen chatting with the younger Abominables at length. One reporter overheard them discussing their favorite websites, cell phones, music, and movies. It has been rumored the Abominables (and many of their relatives) will lead a normal (normal in human terms) life living in Skagway. Finally, this myth has been put to rest; it is no longer a question of whether or not the strange and fearsome Abominable Snowmen-people exist, because now they live among us.

Scar Reporter

SNOW -MAN SUPER DIET?

You're not going to lose weight eating what an Abominable does. Their favorite meal of ice cream, sardines, and pancakes average an incredible 7400 calories a serving! Bon appetit!

About the Breges

Author Karen Bell-Brege just happens to be married to the famous illustrator, Darrin M. Brege. This is their seventh book together, and their fifth in the bestselling Mick Morris Myth Solver series with Five Ways to Finish.™

Karen is a comic and public speaker, as well as the director of an improv comedy troupe. Darrin is also a comic and a radio personality. He has created hundreds of illustrations for major corporations, as well as picture books and movie posters. He is also the original cover artist for another popular series.

The Breges have one son – whose name is Mick! They live in a funky, old townhouse in the Midwest and they love to laugh and have fun! On rainy nights they love sit around making up crazy, scary stories!

Would you like the Breges to visit your school? They have an awesome presentation that will keep you laughing while you learn about art, writing, and reading!

Just have your teacher or school administrator contact their office at (248) 890-5363, or email mickmorrisinfo@yahoo.com for more information on their special presentation!

"Westwood students had the privilege of being visited by authors this spring. Karen and Darrin Brege held two assemblies during Reading Week. The Breges promised and delivered high-energy, interactive performances which included drawing, reading, and writing mixed with humor and comedy. We couldn't have asked for better assemblies."

Published June 10th, 2007 by the Lansing State Journal (www.lsj.com)